SO NORMAL

(A Faith Bold Mystery —Book Four)

BLAKE PIERCE

Blake Pierce

Blake Pierce is the USA Today bestselling author of the RILEY PAGE mystery series, which includes seventeen books. Blake Pierce is also the author of the MACKENZIE WHITE mystery series, comprising fourteen books; of the AVERY BLACK mystery series, comprising six books; of the KERI LOCKE mystery series, comprising five books; of the MAKING OF RILEY PAIGE mystery series, comprising six books; of the KATE WISE mystery series, comprising seven books; of the CHLOE FINE psychological suspense mystery, comprising six books; of the JESSIE HUNT psychological suspense thriller series, comprising twenty-eight books; of the AU PAIR psychological suspense thriller series, comprising three books; of the ZOE PRIME mystery series, comprising six books; of the ADELE SHARP mystery series, comprising sixteen books, of the EUROPEAN VOYAGE cozy mystery series, comprising six books; of the LAURA FROST FBI suspense thriller, comprising eleven books; of the ELLA DARK FBI suspense thriller, comprising fourteen books (and counting); of the A YEAR IN EUROPE cozy mystery series, comprising nine books, of the AVA GOLD mystery series, comprising six books; of the RACHEL GIFT mystery series, comprising ten books (and counting); of the VALERIE LAW mystery series, comprising nine books (and counting); of the PAIGE KING mystery series, comprising eight books (and counting); of the MAY MOORE mystery series, comprising eleven books; of the CORA SHIELDS mystery series, comprising eight books (and counting); of the NICKY LYONS mystery series, comprising eight books (and counting), of the CAMI LARK mystery series, comprising eight books (and counting), of the AMBER YOUNG mystery series, comprising five books (and counting), of the DAISY FORTUNE mystery series, comprising five books (and counting), of the FIONA RED mystery series, comprising eight books (and counting), of the FAITH BOLD mystery series, comprising eight books (and counting), of the JULIETTE HART mystery series, comprising five books (and counting), of the MORGAN CROSS mystery series, comprising five books (and counting), and of the new FINN WRIGHT mystery series, comprising five books (and counting).

An avid reader and lifelong fan of the mystery and thriller genres, Blake loves to hear from you, so please feel free to visit www.blakepierceauthor.com to learn more and stay in touch.

ISBN: 978-1-0943-8207-4

BOOKS BY BLAKE PIERCE

FINN WRIGHT MYSTERY SERIES
WHEN YOU'RE MINE (Book #1)
WHEN YOU'RE SAFE (Book #2)
WHEN YOU'RE CLOSE (Book #3)
WHEN YOU'RE SLEEPING (Book #4)
WHEN YOU'RE SANE (Book #5)

MORGAN CROSS MYSTERY SERIES
FOR YOU (Book #1)
FOR RAGE (Book #2)
FOR LUST (Book #3)
FOR WRATH (Book #4)
FOREVER (Book #5)

JULIETTE HART MYSTERY SERIES
NOTHING TO FEAR (Book #1)
NOTHING THERE (Book #2)
NOTHING WATCHING (Book #3)
NOTHING HIDING (Book #4)
NOTHING LEFT (Book #5)

FAITH BOLD MYSTERY SERIES
SO LONG (Book #1)
SO COLD (Book #2)
SO SCARED (Book #3)
SO NORMAL (Book #4)
SO FAR GONE (Book #5)
SO LOST (Book #6)
SO ALONE (Book #7)
SO FORGOTTEN (Book #8)

FIONA RED MYSTERY SERIES
LET HER GO (Book #1)
LET HER BE (Book #2)
LET HER HOPE (Book #3)
LET HER WISH (Book #4)

LET HER LIVE (Book #5)
LET HER RUN (Book #6)
LET HER HIDE (Book #7)
LET HER BELIEVE (Book #8)

DAISY FORTUNE MYSTERY SERIES
NEED YOU (Book #1)
CLAIM YOU (Book #2)
CRAVE YOU (Book #3)
CHOOSE YOU (Book #4)
CHASE YOU (Book #5)

AMBER YOUNG MYSTERY SERIES
ABSENT PITY (Book #1)
ABSENT REMORSE (Book #2)
ABSENT FEELING (Book #3)
ABSENT MERCY (Book #4)
ABSENT REASON (Book #5)

CAMI LARK MYSTERY SERIES
JUST ME (Book #1)
JUST OUTSIDE (Book #2)
JUST RIGHT (Book #3)
JUST FORGET (Book #4)
JUST ONCE (Book #5)
JUST HIDE (Book #6)
JUST NOW (Book #7)
JUST HOPE (Book #8)

NICKY LYONS MYSTERY SERIES
ALL MINE (Book #1)
ALL HIS (Book #2)
ALL HE SEES (Book #3)
ALL ALONE (Book #4)
ALL FOR ONE (Book #5)
ALL HE TAKES (Book #6)
ALL FOR ME (Book #7)
ALL IN (Book #8)

CORA SHIELDS MYSTERY SERIES
UNDONE (Book #1)

UNWANTED (Book #2)
UNHINGED (Book #3)
UNSAID (Book #4)
UNGLUED (Book #5)
UNSTABLE (Book #6)
UNKNOWN (Book #7)
UNAWARE (Book #8)

MAY MOORE SUSPENSE THRILLER
NEVER RUN (Book #1)
NEVER TELL (Book #2)
NEVER LIVE (Book #3)
NEVER HIDE (Book #4)
NEVER FORGIVE (Book #5)
NEVER AGAIN (Book #6)
NEVER LOOK BACK (Book #7)
NEVER FORGET (Book #8)
NEVER LET GO (Book #9)
NEVER PRETEND (Book #10)
NEVER HESITATE (Book #11)

PAIGE KING MYSTERY SERIES
THE GIRL HE PINED (Book #1)
THE GIRL HE CHOSE (Book #2)
THE GIRL HE TOOK (Book #3)
THE GIRL HE WISHED (Book #4)
THE GIRL HE CROWNED (Book #5)
THE GIRL HE WATCHED (Book #6)
THE GIRL HE WANTED (Book #7)
THE GIRL HE CLAIMED (Book #8)

VALERIE LAW MYSTERY SERIES
NO MERCY (Book #1)
NO PITY (Book #2)
NO FEAR (Book #3)
NO SLEEP (Book #4)
NO QUARTER (Book #5)
NO CHANCE (Book #6)
NO REFUGE (Book #7)
NO GRACE (Book #8)
NO ESCAPE (Book #9)

RACHEL GIFT MYSTERY SERIES
HER LAST WISH (Book #1)
HER LAST CHANCE (Book #2)
HER LAST HOPE (Book #3)
HER LAST FEAR (Book #4)
HER LAST CHOICE (Book #5)
HER LAST BREATH (Book #6)
HER LAST MISTAKE (Book #7)
HER LAST DESIRE (Book #8)
HER LAST REGRET (Book #9)
HER LAST HOUR (Book #10)

AVA GOLD MYSTERY SERIES
CITY OF PREY (Book #1)
CITY OF FEAR (Book #2)
CITY OF BONES (Book #3)
CITY OF GHOSTS (Book #4)
CITY OF DEATH (Book #5)
CITY OF VICE (Book #6)

A YEAR IN EUROPE
A MURDER IN PARIS (Book #1)
DEATH IN FLORENCE (Book #2)
VENGEANCE IN VIENNA (Book #3)
A FATALITY IN SPAIN (Book #4)

ELLA DARK FBI SUSPENSE THRILLER
GIRL, ALONE (Book #1)
GIRL, TAKEN (Book #2)
GIRL, HUNTED (Book #3)
GIRL, SILENCED (Book #4)
GIRL, VANISHED (Book 5)
GIRL ERASED (Book #6)
GIRL, FORSAKEN (Book #7)
GIRL, TRAPPED (Book #8)
GIRL, EXPENDABLE (Book #9)
GIRL, ESCAPED (Book #10)
GIRL, HIS (Book #11)
GIRL, LURED (Book #12)
GIRL, MISSING (Book #13)

GIRL, UNKNOWN (Book #14)

LAURA FROST FBI SUSPENSE THRILLER

ALREADY GONE (Book #1)
ALREADY SEEN (Book #2)
ALREADY TRAPPED (Book #3)
ALREADY MISSING (Book #4)
ALREADY DEAD (Book #5)
ALREADY TAKEN (Book #6)
ALREADY CHOSEN (Book #7)
ALREADY LOST (Book #8)
ALREADY HIS (Book #9)
ALREADY LURED (Book #10)
ALREADY COLD (Book #11)

EUROPEAN VOYAGE COZY MYSTERY SERIES

MURDER (AND BAKLAVA) (Book #1)
DEATH (AND APPLE STRUDEL) (Book #2)
CRIME (AND LAGER) (Book #3)
MISFORTUNE (AND GOUDA) (Book #4)
CALAMITY (AND A DANISH) (Book #5)
MAYHEM (AND HERRING) (Book #6)

ADELE SHARP MYSTERY SERIES

LEFT TO DIE (Book #1)
LEFT TO RUN (Book #2)
LEFT TO HIDE (Book #3)
LEFT TO KILL (Book #4)
LEFT TO MURDER (Book #5)
LEFT TO ENVY (Book #6)
LEFT TO LAPSE (Book #7)
LEFT TO VANISH (Book #8)
LEFT TO HUNT (Book #9)
LEFT TO FEAR (Book #10)
LEFT TO PREY (Book #11)
LEFT TO LURE (Book #12)
LEFT TO CRAVE (Book #13)
LEFT TO LOATHE (Book #14)
LEFT TO HARM (Book #15)
LEFT TO RUIN (Book #16)

THE AU PAIR SERIES

ALMOST GONE (Book#1)
ALMOST LOST (Book #2)
ALMOST DEAD (Book #3)

ZOE PRIME MYSTERY SERIES

FACE OF DEATH (Book#1)
FACE OF MURDER (Book #2)
FACE OF FEAR (Book #3)
FACE OF MADNESS (Book #4)
FACE OF FURY (Book #5)
FACE OF DARKNESS (Book #6)

A JESSIE HUNT PSYCHOLOGICAL SUSPENSE SERIES

THE PERFECT WIFE (Book #1)
THE PERFECT BLOCK (Book #2)
THE PERFECT HOUSE (Book #3)
THE PERFECT SMILE (Book #4)
THE PERFECT LIE (Book #5)
THE PERFECT LOOK (Book #6)
THE PERFECT AFFAIR (Book #7)
THE PERFECT ALIBI (Book #8)
THE PERFECT NEIGHBOR (Book #9)
THE PERFECT DISGUISE (Book #10)
THE PERFECT SECRET (Book #11)
THE PERFECT FAÇADE (Book #12)
THE PERFECT IMPRESSION (Book #13)
THE PERFECT DECEIT (Book #14)
THE PERFECT MISTRESS (Book #15)
THE PERFECT IMAGE (Book #16)
THE PERFECT VEIL (Book #17)
THE PERFECT INDISCRETION (Book #18)
THE PERFECT RUMOR (Book #19)
THE PERFECT COUPLE (Book #20)
THE PERFECT MURDER (Book #21)
THE PERFECT HUSBAND (Book #22)
THE PERFECT SCANDAL (Book #23)
THE PERFECT MASK (Book #24)
THE PERFECT RUSE (Book #25)
THE PERFECT VENEER (Book #26)
THE PERFECT PEOPLE (Book #27)

THE PERFECT WITNESS (Book #28)

CHLOE FINE PSYCHOLOGICAL SUSPENSE SERIES

NEXT DOOR (Book #1)

A NEIGHBOR'S LIE (Book #2)

CUL DE SAC (Book #3)

SILENT NEIGHBOR (Book #4)

HOMECOMING (Book #5)

TINTED WINDOWS (Book #6)

KATE WISE MYSTERY SERIES

IF SHE KNEW (Book #1)

IF SHE SAW (Book #2)

IF SHE RAN (Book #3)

IF SHE HID (Book #4)

IF SHE FLED (Book #5)

IF SHE FEARED (Book #6)

IF SHE HEARD (Book #7)

THE MAKING OF RILEY PAIGE SERIES

WATCHING (Book #1)

WAITING (Book #2)

LURING (Book #3)

TAKING (Book #4)

STALKING (Book #5)

KILLING (Book #6)

RILEY PAIGE MYSTERY SERIES

ONCE GONE (Book #1)

ONCE TAKEN (Book #2)

ONCE CRAVED (Book #3)

ONCE LURED (Book #4)

ONCE HUNTED (Book #5)

ONCE PINED (Book #6)

ONCE FORSAKEN (Book #7)

ONCE COLD (Book #8)

ONCE STALKED (Book #9)

ONCE LOST (Book #10)

ONCE BURIED (Book #11)

ONCE BOUND (Book #12)

ONCE TRAPPED (Book #13)

ONCE DORMANT (Book #14)
ONCE SHUNNED (Book #15)
ONCE MISSED (Book #16)
ONCE CHOSEN (Book #17)

MACKENZIE WHITE MYSTERY SERIES
BEFORE HE KILLS (Book #1)
BEFORE HE SEES (Book #2)
BEFORE HE COVETS (Book #3)
BEFORE HE TAKES (Book #4)
BEFORE HE NEEDS (Book #5)
BEFORE HE FEELS (Book #6)
BEFORE HE SINS (Book #7)
BEFORE HE HUNTS (Book #8)
BEFORE HE PREYS (Book #9)
BEFORE HE LONGS (Book #10)
BEFORE HE LAPSES (Book #11)
BEFORE HE ENVIES (Book #12)
BEFORE HE STALKS (Book #13)
BEFORE HE HARMS (Book #14)

AVERY BLACK MYSTERY SERIES
CAUSE TO KILL (Book #1)
CAUSE TO RUN (Book #2)
CAUSE TO HIDE (Book #3)
CAUSE TO FEAR (Book #4)
CAUSE TO SAVE (Book #5)
CAUSE TO DREAD (Book #6)

KERI LOCKE MYSTERY SERIES
A TRACE OF DEATH (Book #1)
A TRACE OF MURDER (Book #2)
A TRACE OF VICE (Book #3)
A TRACE OF CRIME (Book #4)
A TRACE OF HOPE (Book #5)

PROLOGUE

Kylie glanced over at the bench. The strange man still—he was there before she arrived to work this morning.

"Is that mine?"

Kylie turned her attention away from the bench and its strange occupant. She smiled and handed the guest his latte. This one, like so many other middle-aged men who passed through the subway terminal every day, thought it would be charming to call her sweetheart instead of by her name, despite the fact that her name was clearly printed on her nametag. At least this one didn't also feel a need to ogle her breasts before walking off.

Kylie didn't mind the job so much. She got to work by herself, which suited her just fine. She worked the morning shift, which meant her day was exceedingly busy during the morning rush and very busy during the lunch rush but fairly slow in between. With no supervisor to invent work for her and a very small coffee cart that was easy to clean and maintain, the work wasn't all that hard, and so far, none of the men had done more than ogle her, which was annoying but not bad enough to ruin the job for her.

And the terminal was a great place for people watching. Someone had once called the city a great melting pot, and she found that to be true. People of all shapes, sizes, colors, and creeds passed by every day. Kylie wasn't some great social activist, but she found the eclectic mix of travelers entertaining.

Today, her entertainment was provided by the older man sitting on a nearby bench. He wore a trench coat and an old hat like the ones detectives wore in those old crime movies her grandparents liked to watch. He wore round sunglasses with gold wire rims and sat with the hat pulled down low and the collars of his coat turned up. He looked like a caricature of a spy.

What caught Kylie's eye wasn't his fantastic dress but the way he held his right hand. It rested against his shoulder with the palm lifted up and his fingers curled as though he was holding a martini glass, although his hand was empty.

She watched him for a while, but he stayed where he was. Maybe he was sleeping.

The day wore on, and Kylie forgot about the man. She cleaned the cart, stocked the condiments, and when that was done, worked a little on her homework while she awaited the lunch rush. The lunch rush came, and with it the only slightly smaller crowd of businesspeople and students navigating the underground routes between the city and the spiderweb of urban and suburban sprawl that surrounded the city center.

She finished her shift, and just as the lunch rush was winding down, Louis arrived to take over for her. They exchanged the usual pleasantries and then Kylie left him and started toward the platform.

She glanced over at the bench and saw that the strange man was still sitting there. Exactly there. His hand was still casually holding his invisible martini. She stared at him incredulously. How could he still be asleep? She had been here for eight hours! It was like he was …

She felt a chill creep through her, and she turned quickly away. She walked to her platform, but the chill spread until it became an icy hand that gripped her heart. She wanted desperately to ignore it, but she couldn't push it away.

She glanced at the clock. One fifty-two. Her train would arrive in three minutes. She didn't have time to deal with this.

Then again, it didn't make sense for him to sit at a bench across from her cart all day. He could be hurt or sick. Or he could be stalking her. She stared at him over her shoulder, but he continued to stare straight ahead, his hand held at that awkward angle.

She started to walk away again but stopped. She tried to tell herself that she should just ignore him, but the nagging in her mind had become a dull roar that grew less dull and more of a roar every second.

Heart pounding, she turned and walked slowly back to the stranger. When she approached him, she swallowed and called, "Hello? Sir?"

The stranger didn't so much as twitch. She called again and got the same answer. Then she called a third time. Then a fourth.

He's sleeping, she told herself. *He's sleeping, and I should leave him be.*

But she couldn't leave. She had to know. She reached forward, hand trembling, and called a final time, "Sir?"

She shook him gently. His hand flopped to his side. His head lolled forward, and his sunglasses fell off. He stared ahead with vacant, glazed eyes, and Kylie knew.

She jumped backward, shrieking as the dead man slid lazily off the bench and fell face first on the ground.

CHAPTER ONE

Faith thought for a moment before answering. The question was one she had asked herself many times, but now that someone else asked, she was no longer sure of the answer.

Doctor West waited patiently, his piercing, gray-blue eyes moderated by his soft, kind smile. Faith took a breath and gave it her best shot. "Umm … I think the worst part was that I couldn't help but scream. I mean, I knew I was caught, and that was terrible. I knew I was going to die, and that wasn't fun, obviously, but I thought that I could at least keep from screaming. I didn't want to give him the satisfaction of hearing me react to the pain."

"Hmm," Doctor West said, "so, it was the loss of control that you found the hardest?"

Faith stared at Doctor West in amazement. She had played that scene over and over in her mind at least a dozen times a day since Trammell had captured and tortured her, to say nothing of her near-constant nightmares, and not once had she thought of her reaction in that way. Hearing him say it made her realize that he was exactly right. For the first time in her life, she was in control of nothing, not even her own mind.

"Yes," she said. "Yes, that's exactly it. I mean, I was a Marine. Not to perpetuate a stereotype, but Marines really do believe we're the toughest and strongest people in the world. Not to perpetuate another stereotype, but as a woman, I had to be tougher and stronger than the men I was with. I had to fight harder, push further, and give less, and I did. I was the first one to the fight and the last one out of it. That didn't change when I joined the FBI. I had to push so hard to get any kind of respect as a field agent, and I earned it every step of the way. Any challenge I faced, I overcame, so finding myself in a situation where I just couldn't overcome, where every ounce of toughness and resilience and strength I had was utterly stripped away, and I was …"

Her voice trailed off. Tears welled in her eyes, but she fought them back. "I always imagined that if I died in a situation like that, I would die with my head held high and a snarl on my face. Instead, I died—or nearly died—screaming and weeping like a little girl."

Doctor West regarded her a moment, then said, “You mentioned twice that you believe you had to work harder to achieve success than your male colleagues. Do you feel you are or were treated differently because of your gender?”

“Oh, constantly,” Faith said. “Not by everyone but by most people. There’s the typical testosterone-fueled bullshit, especially in the Corps: men trying to impress me by saying they’ll take care of me or showing off how tough or strong they are. That doesn’t bother me too much. Men are notoriously awful at behaving around a woman they’re attracted to.”

Doctor West smiled at that.

“What does bother me is when people assume that I’m less capable or less emotionally stable because I’m a woman. I still deal with colleagues talking—not down to me, but like they have to change the way they phrase things so that my female mind can grasp it or being extra sensitive about certain subjects because I can’t handle the nitty-gritty stuff. Even friends will behave like I’m some emotional basket case they need to manage, or I’ll screw everything up with my emotionality.”

“You’re referring to your partner, Agent Prince?”

Faith sighed. “Yeah. Just a few weeks ago, we were on that case in Tucson, and he … basically suggested that since the Donkey Killer, I’ve been losing my grip on my emotions, and that it’s been affecting my ability to do my job.”

“Why do you feel he said that to you?”

Faith sighed again. “I think he’s worried about me. I don’t blame him. I mean, it’s hard to see someone you care about get hurt. I’m sure he relives the moment he walked in on Trammell hurting me every day just like I relive being hurt. I just wish he would stop treating me like I’m …” she lifted her hands, looking for the right words, “… damaged goods, and he needs to monitor me or treat me with kid gloves because I’ve suffered.”

“So, you don’t think there’s any truth to the claim that your trauma has affected you on the job?”

“I don’t,” Faith said confidently. “I’ve solved three high-profile cases since that event. In all three of those cases, I’ve gotten into a physical altercation with the subjects and been able to affect the arrest regardless. I mean, not by myself. I had my K9 unit and my partner with me, but I handled myself well.”

"Hmm," he said, "I find it interesting that you felt a need to point out that you overpowered your suspects physically. Do you feel that perhaps the experience of being overpowered by Trammell has caused you to seek out physical confrontation as a means to prove to yourself that you are still capable of doing your job?"

Faith once more felt stunned. She didn't agree with Doctor West, but she was suddenly unsure if she really didn't agree with him or if she just didn't want to agree with him.

The doctor's cell phone beeped, and he said, "Ah. Well, I suppose you escape that question today."

He smiled charmingly, and Faith chuckled in spite of herself. "We'll reapproach that question next week. In the meantime, Faith, I encourage you to try to accept the feelings you're having, even the ones that seem destructive. The way to overcome trauma is to face it. That can be hard, and it invariably requires us to admit truths that are uncomfortable, but the end result is worth it."

Faith smiled at him. "Thank you, Doctor West. I'll try."

"That's all any of us can do," he said.

He stood, extending his hand to Faith. She took it and thanked him one last time before leaving his office.

When she reached her car, she took a deep breath and released it slowly. She felt good, far more relaxed than usual. She hated to admit it, but talking to Doctor West was actually helping. The tension that seemed to hover over her like a dark cloud was gradually receding. Granted, this was only her third session, and they had only just started to dive into the heart of things, but she didn't feel the frustration she expected to feel with the process. Doctor West was as pedantic as any psychologist she had met, but he seemed to genuinely care. It surprised Faith to realize how much that meant to her.

She started to drive home, but the farther she drove from Doctor West's office, the more the session receded and the more the case came back to the forefront.

The case wasn't hers. In fact, multiple people had made it abundantly clear to her that the case wasn't hers, and she needed to stay away.

Still, it was hers. It should be hers. She had suffered from the Donkey Killer, but she was also the agent most knowledgeable about him. There was someone out there killing people the same way, and she needed to be the one to bring him to justice.

She had tried to investigate the most recent murder using her connections with the coroner's office, but Clark—one of the agents assigned to the case—had waylaid her and warned her off. She needed a different angle.

She texted David that she would be home a little late and headed to the former home of Brenda Fiero, the latest victim of the copycat killer. She was an important victim because instead of being killed in an abandoned barn or farmhouse miles from civilization, she was killed in a public-school gymnasium and left there to be found, brutally mutilated and tortured.

She reached the house ten minutes later. An older woman of about sixty—Brenda's mother, Faith guessed—answered the door.

"Good afternoon," Faith said, "I'm Special Agent Faith Bold of the FBI. I'm investigating your daughter's murder. I was wondering if I could ask you a few questions?"

"Oh," the woman said. "I'm sorry, no."

Faith blinked. "Is this a bad time?"

"No," the woman said. She shifted on her feet uncomfortably. "I'm … I'm afraid I've been told not to talk to you."

Faith stared at her, stunned. "You've been told not to talk to me? By who?"

"The other agent I spoke to," she said, avoiding Faith's eyes. "He told me that there was an agent who was unlawfully impeding his investigation and if she was to speak to me, not to answer any questions."

Faith was speechless. She knew Clark was unhappy with her snooping around, but to go out of his way to tell the family not to talk to her? Brenda had died prior to Faith's encounter with Clark at the coroner's office, so he had either told the family this before that interaction or he had called them after the fact to inform them of Faith's involvement.

"I'm sorry to hear that," she said. "I assure you, I'm not here to interfere, I'm here to help. I believe I have a skill set that could provide valuable insight to this investigation."

"Are you saying your colleagues aren't skilled?" she asked.

"No," Faith said. "Not at all. I just want to help. Don't you want as many people looking for your daughter's killer as possible."

The older woman hesitated, but Faith could tell her hesitation wasn't because she was swayed by Faith's argument but because she was trying to think of a way to get Faith to leave her porch. Finally, she said, “I think I’m happy with Agents Clark and Desrouleaux. I don’t want too many cooks in the kitchen, and they’re officially assigned to the case.”

Faith took a breath. “I see.” She handed the older woman a card. “Well, if you change your mind, please give me a call. I assure you, my interest in this case is perfectly professional.”

She nodded, but Faith could tell she wasn’t convinced. Faith felt irritation rise but forced it down. Her anger was at Clark, not an innocent woman barely a month past losing her daughter.

She smiled and started to leave when the older woman said, “He also told me to call him if you tried to speak to me.”

Faith turned back and met the woman’s eyes. She quickly looked away from Faith, once more shifting her feet. Faith forced a smile and kept her tone pleasant as she said, “Well, if you can refrain from calling him, that would help me a lot.”

The woman nodded and said, “Sure. I won’t call.”

She still didn’t meet Faith’s eyes, though, and Faith decided odds were better than even that she would call Clark the moment her car pulled away. Well, there was nothing she could do about that now. She smiled again and said, “Have a nice day, ma’am.”

She got into her car and took another deep breath, but this time, she didn’t relax when she released it. She texted David to let her know that she was on her way home a little earlier than expected and would see him in twenty minutes.

“Dammit,” she said softly. “Goddammit.”

Clark’s persistence in keeping Faith from the case was an unexpected problem. She and Clark had always gotten along. He was one of the few of Faith’s colleagues who had never treated her differently for being a woman and one of the even fewer colleagues who seemed free of the competitive streak that was almost ubiquitous among FBI agents.

He had even told her that he and Desrouleaux had recommended to the Boss that Faith be assigned to the case and expressed remorse that the Boss had disagreed. Faith knew he wouldn’t actively help her in the pursuit of the case, but if he truly believed Faith was the right agent for the job, then he should be grateful for her help. He could allow her to investigate and just get information from her that would help him. She wanted to be the one to catch this guy, but she didn’t care if anyone knew. Clark could take the credit for all she cared.

So, why was he suddenly actively hindering her?

She sighed and cursed under her breath again. Her knuckles tightened over the steering wheel, and she took deep breaths, holding them for several seconds and releasing them slowly. The breathing exercises didn't take her anger away, but they soothed the physical tension so that she was gradually able to relax her grip and release the tension in her shoulders.

She would still solve this case. That wasn't a question. She would still solve this case, but Clark's interference had just made everything that much harder.

She could almost hear the copycat killer laughing at her as he prepared to carve yet another victim. "Dammit," she whispered again. How many more people needed to die before the Boss just let her solve the case?

Her hands tightened over the steering wheel again, and this time, she didn't try the breathing exercises.

CHAPTER TWO

Turk leapt into her arms the moment she walked in the door. He began licking her face exuberantly, and Faith twisted her head away, laughing and pushing him down. "Turk!" she cried. "Not the face!"

"Sorry about that," David said sheepishly. "I let him kiss my face, and now he thinks that's how you greet someone you love."

"Well," Faith said, finally succeeding in getting Turk back onto all fours, "he's not wrong. I just wish that rule applied to humans only."

"Oh, come on," David said, taking her in his arms. "Dog kisses aren't all that bad."

He leaned down to kiss her, but Faith turned her head and pushed him away. "Uh uh," she said, "we're *both* brushing our teeth before there's any kissing."

David smiled and said, "Fair enough. Hey, I was thinking we could try dinner at that new Indian place down the street."

"Oh, I'm sorry," Faith said. "I told Michael I would have dinner with him and Ellie tonight."

"Oh," David said, lifting his eyebrows. "Tonight's the night, huh?"

"Yep," Faith said, "I get to be the awkward ex meeting the new girl. You know, you could come with me, if you want."

He smiled apologetically. "I would love to, but my friend from veterinary school flies in tonight, and I promised to pick him up."

"And enjoy some drinks and debauchery on the town, no doubt," Faith said with a mischievous smile.

David laughed. "Well, drinks, yes, but no debauchery." He offered a mischievous smile of his own and said, "Unless you want me to come over after you're finished with Michael and Ellie."

Faith chuckled. "I think I'll take a raincheck on the debauchery for tonight but thank you." David's face fell exaggeratedly, and Faith rolled her eyes. "Don't try the puppy dog act with me. I can tell when you're lying."

"What's wrong with puppy dogs?" David asked, grinning and lifting his hands.

Turk whined in agreement.

Faith smiled and kissed David softly. When she pulled away, she said, "Absolutely nothing."

David's eyes furrowed slightly, but he kept his grin. "I thought you said no more kissing until we brush our teeth."

"You're right," Faith said, pulling away. "I won't kiss you anymore."

He pulled her to him and kissed her deeply. Her senses came alive, and she melted into his arms. Her hands snaked behind his neck, and—

He pulled away suddenly, leaving her gasping. She glared at him, heat warming her cheeks, and he laughed and kissed her on the tip of her nose. "I'll see you later, then."

"Later," she said.

***

That kiss remained with Faith as she drove to Michael's house. A month ago, David had asked her if she saw a future with him. She had freaked out and basically taken advantage of the Tucson case to ghost him for a few days. When she did talk to him, she skirted around the edge of his question until she got back to Philadelphia where he reassured her that he only wanted to know if there was a chance at a future and wasn't looking for a commitment right now.

At the time, Faith had been relieved. She liked David, but she was nowhere near ready to even consider a future with anyone. Now, after talking with Doctor West, she thought she might be. Not right away. She still had a long way to go before she recovered from the effects of her trauma at Trammell's hands, but she believed now that she could recover one day, and when she did, there would be nothing preventing her from moving things along with David.

Except the copycat killer case. Faith's smile faded. She wanted to move on from Trammell, but she couldn't as long as that copycat killer was out there doing to people what Trammell had done to her. She couldn't just stand aside and watch while Clark and Desrouleaux continually screwed up the investigation.

She needed to solve that case. If she could put the copycat killer behind bars, she could once and for all move on from the original Donkey Killer and what he had done to her. She could have a future with David. She could have a future with herself.

Turk barked, jolting her from her thoughts. She narrowly managed to avoid hitting a semi that changed lanes in front of her with her in his blind spot.

"Jesus," she muttered. "Thanks, boy."

Turk barked, and Faith could swear she heard sarcasm in the sound.

"Do you want to drive?" she asked.

Turk snorted, and Faith said, "Yeah, yeah, right back at ya, buddy."

They reached Michael's house ten minutes later. It was an old, brownstone townhouse in the early twentieth century New York style. Michael said it reminded him of some detective novel or other he used to read. Faith thought it looked like the house a serial killer might live in if serial killers were all as they were portrayed in Hollywood. She mentioned this to Michael once, and he had stared blankly at her.

"David laughed," she said as she pulled her old Crown Victoria to a stop. The venerable, old Windsor V8 grumbled appreciatively to a standstill, and she patted the dash before stepping out. The car probably had two years of life left, maybe three if she babied it. Then she would have to give in and buy a newer vehicle. Not much newer. New cars were too posh for her taste. Even cheap economy cars felt to Faith like they glided over a cushion of air instead of rumbling powerfully over the road. Where was the fun in that? Give her an old, powerful American sedan over a cheap, foreign tin can with a lawnmower engine any day.

She walked to the door and steeled herself for what she was sure would be the most uncomfortable dinner of her life. She and Michael had argued over his new girlfriend a few times before settling into an uneasy silence on the subject.

Ellie was married. Separated for two years now, but still married and seemingly no closer to divorce than she was when she met Michael five months ago. Faith saw red flag after red flag, but Michael was in love, and when you see things through rose colored glasses, it's hard to see red flags.

Well, she would leave him to his business. Besides, as far as she knew, Michael was right, and Ellie's financial situation was complicated and prevented her from simply leaving cleanly.

Not that it mattered tonight. She was Faith the supportive friend tonight, not Faith the investigator.

The door opened, and she smiled, "Hi, Michael."

He looked her up and down, "What's with the clown smile?" he asked. "Jesus, she's my girlfriend, not Internal Affairs."

Faith rolled her eyes and pushed past him. Turk offered a polite bark in greeting and followed her inside.

A petite, blonde woman about four inches shorter than Faith's five-foot-eight stood up from her seat on the couch and offered Faith a nervous smile. She had big, expressive, blue eyes and an innocent expression that Faith knew instantly had won Michael over at first sight.

Faith smiled, trying her best not to look like a clown, and extended her hand. "Hi," she said, "you must be Ellie."

"And you must be Faith," the blonde said with a nervous chuckle. She took Faith's hand in her own and squeezed too hard, another sign that she was nervous.

God, was she that intimidated? What had Michael told her?

It occurred to Faith with a sudden flash of fear that he might have told Ellie of their argument about her. Faith wouldn't put it past him. Michael was a sharer, especially when he was in love. Faith knew all about that.

Ellie turned to Turk and beamed. "And you must be Turk! Oh, Michael's told me all about you."

She reached forward to pet Turk, and Turk growled low in his throat. Ellie jerked her hand backward, and Faith said, "Hey! Stop it!"

Turk looked at her and stopped growling, but when he looked back at Ellie, his eyes retained a wary expression.

"It's just because he doesn't know you yet," Michael explained. "K9s sometimes have trouble adjusting to new faces. Right Faith?"

He offered Faith a smile that stopped below his eyes. Faith nodded and said, "Oh yes. Sorry, I should have warned you. He'll come around."

Michael nodded approvingly and relaxed. Ellie looked at Faith again and said, "Wow. You're beautiful. No wonder Michael liked you."

Faith looked away and cleared her throat. Michael sighed, and Faith could see him prepare himself for a night that would be just as awkward as Faith's. Ellie blushed beet red and looked mortified. "I'm so sorry. I don't know why I said that. Umm. Welcome to our humble abode!"

"Thank you," Faith said.

She looked questioningly at Michael, and Michael said, "Ellie moved in with me last week. We figured that there was no need for her to spend money renting that apartment when she's in the middle of a divorce."

"Michael," Ellie said, reddening, "we don't need to talk about that."

"You're right," Michael said. "Sorry about that. Anyway, she's here, and here is ours now. Thank you for coming over, Faith. Ellie's been wanting to meet you for months."

Ellie's smile told Faith that was the opposite of the truth. Turk continued to watch her warily, and Faith noticed that he stood in front of her protectively, as though Ellie was a threat.

Turk never acted this way around anyone. K9 or not, he was basically a puppy when it came to strangers. She had seen him walk straight up to people he had just met and push his head into their belly for pats. The only time he acted like this was when he was in the presence of a killer.

Well, Ellie wasn't a killer. The woman would probably lose a fight to a good-sized middle schooler.

But she was hiding something. Try as Faith might to avoid thinking that, it was as clear as the cute little button nose on her face that she was lying to Michael and to Faith. That could explain Turk's behavior. He was protective of both Faith and Michael, and typically when someone was lying to them, it was because they were murderers. He probably sensed that Ellie was lying but also sensed that she wasn't a threat, which was why he was suspicious of her but not aggressive.

It's none of my business, Faith told herself. *I'm here as a supportive friend, not a detective.*

They sat down to dinner, and Faith was relieved to see Turk eagerly enjoy the steak Ellie had prepared for him. He relaxed slightly around her, and Faith felt her own suspicions ease.

"So, Ellie," Faith said, "Michael here likes to tell me how pretty and nice you are, but he hasn't told me anything else. So, tell me about yourself."

Ellie reddened. "Oh, um … well, I work in a call center, so it's kind of boring. You know, compared to what *you* guys do."

"Really?" Faith said. "You don't deal with hilariously irritating customers all day?"

Ellie giggled. "Well, I suppose so."

"God," Faith said, shaking her head, "how do you deal with that? I couldn't handle people screaming at me all day."

"People don't scream at you?" Ellie asked.

"Well, yeah, but usually when they do, I get to throw them to the ground and handcuff them."

Ellie giggled, and Faith didn't have to look at Michael to know that girly laugh made him swoon.

The rest of dinner continued in the same vein. Ellie was nervous and shy and when she did talk, she was softspoken and giggly and almost sickeningly sweet. Faith realized uncomfortably that Ellie was nearly the opposite of Faith herself.

She hated that she thought that. She and Michael had spit mutually nearly two years ago and almost a year ago had agreed that they would never be romantic again. She had no interest in Michael, and he had no interest in her, so why did it matter how Ellie compared to Faith?

She realized she was slipping into the detective role again. She couldn't resist the hypothesis that Michael chose Ellie specifically because she was different from Faith. She wasn't sure why that bothered her. It shouldn't bother her. So what if that was the reason? If he was happy, then that was good.

Then again, there was that mysteriously lingering husband to worry about.

No! No more! God, she just needed to get through this one dinner without prying into Michael's personal life.

After dinner, they put on a movie about a mail order bride who leaves New England in 1910 to marry a widower farmer in Kansas who struggles to raise his two children after his wife dies giving birth to the youngest. It was a good movie, but despite her best efforts, Faith found her attention traveling to Ellie.

She leaned against Michael's chest while they sat together on the couch. Michael was clearly enamored with her, looking at her with a fervent, earnest expression that Faith had never seen on his face before, not even when he and Faith believed they were in love.

Ellie occasionally looked up at Michael and smiled at him. They would kiss softly, and on the surface, they looked exactly like two lovers in the first bloom of romance.

Faith's curse was that she could never look only at the surface. Ellie's smile was soft and glowing, but the corners of her mouth were just slightly too stiff. She melted against Michael, but there was the barest hint of tension in her shoulders and arms. Her pose seemed relaxed, but Faith noticed her left foot twitched rhythmically as though she was tapping a rhythm in the air.

Turk sat in front of Faith, his eyes never wavering from her. Faith knew that he was as suspicious as she was, and she realized that he, like her, wasn't entirely sure why.

The movie came to an end, and after a little more small talk, Faith announced it was time for her to leave. Ellie stood and smiled. "It was so great to meet you, Faith."

She leaned forward, arms outstretched for an embrace, and Turk barked sharply and leapt in between them. Ellie jumped back, the blood draining from her face, and Michael jumped protectively in front of her.

"Turk!" Faith cried. "Stop it!"

Her face flushed red with embarrassment. She opened her mouth and started to stammer another apology when Michael's phone rang.

He answered it, his eyes never leaving Faith. "Prince." A pause. "She's here." Another pause. "All right. We're on our way."

He hung up and said, "That was the Boss. New case just dropped." He turned to Ellie, who stood behind him, eyes wide with fear as she looked at Turk. "Sorry, honey."

He looked at Faith and said in a clipped tone. "Let's go. You drive."

Faith followed him out of the house, mortified. She couldn't believe Turk had behaved the way he did. She considered apologizing to Michael but decided to save that for later. He was almost certainly not in the mood to hear it now.

And while she did feel terrible about what happened, her larger concern was why Turk behaved the way he did. His instincts were flawless when it came to people.

What did he see in Ellie that made him feel she was a threat?

CHAPTER THREE

When Faith was sixteen, she attended her junior prom with Freddie Macintosh. Neither of them liked each other. Freddie was an introverted kid who didn't even want to go to the prom and was only going because his parents insisted that he be social. Faith was not at all attracted to Freddie and resented being forced to go with a boy she didn't like instead of just going alone.

She and Freddie had planned to split up when they reached the prom, since Freddie had no interest in Faith either, or any girl for that matter, but Mrs. Macintosh had insisted on chaperoning them "just in case Freddie's hands go somewhere they don't belong."

That was probably still the most uncomfortable drive of her life, but this one was pretty damned close. Twice she opened her mouth to apologize for Turk's behavior, and twice she closed it without saying anything.

Part of her, of course, was mortified, but part of her feared that if she started talking, she wouldn't be able to help pointing out the signs she had noticed, the ones that suggested that Ellie might not be the sweet, perfect princess she seemed. Letting *that* cat out of the bag was probably the worst possible thing she could do.

Finally, they reached the field office, and Faith could breathe a sigh of relief. Then she remembered her encounter with Clark, and her relief faded. If Clark had gone to the Boss, then he would have no problem chastising her in front of Michael and announcing that she was off the case.

The Boss, whose real name was Grant Monroe, was the most decorated Special Agent-In-Charge in the Bureau. At one point, his name had been legendary, up there with Mark Felt, Melvin Purvis, and Joe Pistone. He was considered to be a shoo-in for Director when his time came, but a very heated, very public argument with a Deputy Director had relegated him to a permanent fixture in the Philadelphia Field Office, a punishment Grant took with pride.

To his agents, he was known simply as The Boss, and he wore that title well. He was also a hardass known for his acerbic and impatient demeanor, so the fact that he glared at them like an angry elementary school principal didn't give Faith any indication that he knew about her interference on the copycat case.

"Good, you're here," the Boss said. "Sit down."

They sat, Turk sitting in between the two chairs the agents occupied. The Boss tossed a file on the desk in front of them. Faith opened it, and Michael leaned over to look with her. The first document was an image of a man, dressed rather comically in a trench coat, dark sunglasses, and a wide-brim fedora, lying in the middle of what appeared to be a major subway terminal.

His dress was the only part of the image that was comical. He was sprawled in a position that would only be comfortable if he were past such concerns as physical comfort.

"Chester McIlhenny," the Boss said, "sixty-four. Found dead this afternoon by a barista at the coffee cart in the Twin Cities Terminal."

"We're going to Minneapolis-St. Paul?" Michael asked.

"No, New York," the Boss corrected.

"I thought the Twin Cities were Minneapolis-St. Paul."

"You can bring it up to the Metro Authority when you see them," the Boss said.

"Suspects?" Michael asked.

"None," the Boss said.

Faith raised an eyebrow. "So, this man was dumped there in broad daylight, and no one noticed anyone suspicious?"

"No," the Boss said. "He wasn't dumped. He was staged."

"Staged?" Michael asked.

"Yes," the Boss repeated. "He was set up in that position and left there dead. We're waiting on a report from the coroner, but he was dead at least since early that morning."

"And no one noticed until the barista in the afternoon?" Faith asked.

"I'm sure people noticed him," the Boss said. "He's dressed like Dick Tracy. Just because they noticed he was there doesn't mean they noticed he was dead. People stop there just long enough for coffee, not long enough to go check on the weird guy sitting on a bench who looks like Deep Throat starring Humphrey Bogart."

"So, he was staged early in the morning and left there, not found until the barista gets off work," Michael said. "Anything else we should know?"

"Yes," the Boss said. "He was a juror on the Hornfeldt case."

Faith's eyes widened. August Hornfeldt, colorfully nicknamed Joy Buzzer for his MO of killing people by using an illegally overpowered stun gun, was a serial killer who had terrorized New York for over five years. He moved slowly and methodically, killing only seven people in five years. Unfortunately for him, his last victim was the Police Commissioner's mother. He was captured by NYPD hours later, much to the embarrassment of Special Agent Kapernick, who was currently on paid leave pending reassignment for failing to do for years what the boys in blue did in minutes.

"That explains why this is an FBI case already," Faith said.

"So, we think this is retaliation?" Michael asked.

"We don't think anything, Prince," the Boss said. "You two have an especially bad habit of thinking and acting on those thoughts before taking the time to examine them critically. I encourage both of you to try some good, old-fashioned investigative work before you start arresting everyone who might possibly fit your profile."

"Fair enough," Michael said.

Faith sighed, irritated at the jibe, which she knew was directed more toward her than to Michael. She decided to push back a little.

"We've never charged anyone of a crime they didn't commit, sir. Good, old-fashioned investigative work involves interrogating suspects, even if those suspects often turn out to be dead ends."

"Well, good for you, Bold," the Boss said. "Maybe this time you can use warrants and cooperation instead of smash-and-grab."

Faith didn't have an excuse for that, so she only nodded.

"All right," the Boss said. "Move your asses. New York's an hour and a half away, so you can drive. Go straight to the scene. They want the terminal reopened for the morning rush, so you have very little time to look at the scene before it's gone forever."

***

On the way to the airport, Michael asked the question Faith was afraid he would ask.

"You want to tell me what the hell that was back there?"

She tried hoping the question wasn't the one she thought it was anyway. "You know how the Boss is. Besides, the last two cases meant rubbing shoulders with different departments. He gets irritable when he has to deal with people he can't order to do as he says, and he's probably hoping we don't create that problem for him again."

"Don't bullshit me, Faith!" Michael said.

The words weren't unusual, but the tone was. He wasn't ragging her; he was genuinely angry. She sighed and said, "I don't know, Michael. He's never been that way with anyone before."

"You know she's never going to be comfortable around Turk after that."

"Oh man," Faith said drily. "Does this mean I have to move out?"

"I'm serious, Faith, what's going on?"

"Nothing's going on, Michael! For Christ's sake, it's not a big deal! He wasn't going to attack her."

"It sure looked like he was for a moment."

Faith turned to him and said, "Would you like to ask him? He's sitting right here."

She gestured to Turk, and Turk's ears pricked up as he realized he was being talked about.

"Okay, fair enough," Michael said. "I'll take your word for it. Still, he clearly didn't like her."

"And I'm sorry for that," she said, "but I didn't make him decide not to like her."

"Are you sure about that?" he asked. "The only time I've ever seen him behave that way before is when he thinks someone is a threat to you."

"Well, you know," Faith said, "Ellie is pretty intimidating. I guess I was just afraid she might kick my ass, and Turk picked up on it."

"Sarcasm aside, Faith," Michael said, "he picked up on something."

"Well, maybe you should ask Ellie what that might be," Faith retorted.

"You see, that's what I mean," Michael said. "You don't like her. Why don't you like her?"

"I never said I didn't like her," Faith said.

"Do you like her?" Michael asked directly.

Faith sighed. "It doesn't matter, Michael. You like her. That's what matters."

"It does matter," Michael said. "It matters to me that you like her. How would you feel if I didn't like David?"

"Unless you felt a need to point it out every time we saw each other, I wouldn't think about it, Michael," Faith replied irritably. "That's the truth."

Michael was quiet for a moment. Then he said, "Well, I guess that's just one of the differences between you and me."

Faith sighed. "Look, Michael, can we just forget about it, please? Next time we see each other, I'll have David watch Turk. Ellie never needs to see him again."

"Yes, she does," Michael insisted. "I want to spend the rest of my life with Ellie, and that means I want her to be able to interact with all of my friends, even the furry ones."

Faith couldn't stifle the surprise in her voice. "You're asking her to marry you?"

"Is that a problem?" he asked.

Faith's initial reaction was frustration but before she could repeat that she didn't have a problem with Ellie, her second reaction took over. She recalled the tension in Ellie's body when Michael kissed or touched her, the way she seemed to deflect the conversation away from her husband. The fact was that she *did* have a problem with Ellie, a lot of problems. Now, Michael was planning to marry her, and she wasn't even divorced from her current husband.

She chose her words carefully. "I think you might want to wait until her current marriage is over before you start a new one."

"Her current marriage is over," Michael insisted, "in all but name."

"Well, if you want her to take your last name, then you'll have to wait until she gives up the other guy's," Faith pointed out.

"Oh, she's not taking my name," he said. "We agreed that that's an unnecessary construct that doesn't add anything to a relationship."

Faith turned to him in shock. "So, you've already talked about getting married?"

"Of course," Michael said. "I'm in love with her, and you and I both know that in our line of work, waiting isn't something we can afford."

"I don't know that I agree with that," Faith said. "I mean, when David asked me if I wanted a future with him, I almost broke up with him."

"Yeah, well maybe that's another difference between us," Michael said. "I'm not scared of an emotional connection."

Faith looked at him again. "Is there something you want to say, Michael?" she said brittlely. "Because if you have any lingering resentment toward me over the way our relationship ended, then I'd love to get those feelings out of the way now, so they aren't a problem moving forward."

"I'm not talking about us, Faith. You and I both agreed we weren't right for each other, and we still aren't. I'm only saying that I don't appreciate the constant negativity from you about Ellie."

"I haven't said anything, Michael!" Faith shouted. "You can't accuse me of saying something I didn't say!"

"But it's how you feel," he said, "whether you admit it or not."

"No, it isn't!" Faith insisted. "I'm happy for you!"

"Do you like Ellie?" he asked. "Don't lie to me, Faith."

Faith sighed. Once more, she chose her words carefully. "Michael, she seems nice. She seems sweet. She seems like she truly … I'm sure she likes you. But she's still married to the husband she told you she would leave months ago, and there's no sign of that marriage ending. I know it doesn't mean anything that she doesn't want your last name, but why is she keeping his?"

His eyes darkened, and Faith said, "but like I said, it doesn't matter. I never liked my uncle's new wife, but they've been together for twenty years, and they're happy as hell. You're your own person, Michael, and you're going to have to accept that sometimes you and I are going to have different opinions on things."

"She's not a thing, Faith."

"I know that," she snapped. "I just …"

She let her voice trail off. She didn't want to fight with him over this, but she couldn't promise that she could just ignore the situation. Michael was her friend, and Turk had sensed something in Ellie that concerned him. If it concerned Turk, then it concerned Faith too.

"Forget about it," Michael said. "Let's just drop it. We're on a case. We'll focus on that."

Before Faith could respond, Michael leaned his chair back and pulled his hat down over his eyes. Faith kept her eyes on the road, but despite Michael's exhortation, she couldn't pull her focus away from Ellie.

CHAPTER FOUR

Try as he might, Michael couldn't sleep on the car ride. Part of it was the caffeine from the multiple cups of coffee he'd had. He decided he'd have to try to quit that addiction or at least cut back. Ellie had been bugging him about it for a while now anyway.

Most of the reason, of course, was Faith's attitude toward Ellie and her refusal to talk about it. Michael wasn't stupid. He could tell Faith didn't like her. Faith was excellent at spotting a liar, but that didn't make her any good at lying herself, and Michael could see the tension in Faith's body language and tone of voice at dinner.

He wasn't worried about Turk. Even if Turk hated Ellie, Michael knew that a single word from either of them would stop him from doing anything to her. His behavior at dinner might have frightened Ellie, but she didn't know him. He knew that Turk would never attack anyone without Faith's say-so.

But Faith didn't trust her. He could see that as clearly as he could see Faith didn't like her. It had nothing to do with jealousy. If Faith ever had any true romantic feelings for Michael, those had died a long time ago, and anyway, she was clearly happy with David.

If only Faith would just tell him what bothered her! Then they could talk, and he could convince her that she had nothing to worry about. If she just gave Ellie a chance, she would see that Ellie was a wonderful, sweet human being who was everything Michael had ever needed.

The worst part was that in his deepest heart, Michael shared the same suspicions he believed Faith had. Ellie wouldn't give him a straight answer about the state of her marriage. She would only say things are complicated or that it's difficult right now.

Those were her two favorite words. Complicated and difficult. Those were the answers she gave when she didn't want to answer a question. "Things are complicated right now, Michael." "It's difficult at the moment, Michael." Then, on the rare occasions he did push her for a more specific answer, he would get the famous, "I'm trying Michael, but it's not as simple as it seems."

He accepted those answers because he wanted to. He invited Faith over because he hoped Faith would bond with her, and that by seeing Faith bond with her, he could let go of his doubts. Instead, Faith had become immediately suspicious of her, or rather even more suspicious than she already was.

And dammit, even Turk didn't trust her.

He could no longer hide his own lack of trust. He was grateful for the phone call from the Boss, not only because it allowed him to end the awkward interaction between Faith and Ellie but because it kept him from having to admit his own suspicions.

He wouldn't allow those suspicions to solidify in his mind. In his heart, he still believed Ellie was the one for him. If he told her what he suspected, and he was wrong, then he would lose her, and if he lost her, he couldn't believe he would ever love again.

So, he just told himself that Faith was the one with the problem, not Ellie. Then he told himself that it didn't matter who was the problem because they were on a case, and everything else could wait.

"We're here."

Michael lifted his hat off of his face and didn't bother hiding the fact that he wasn't really asleep. He got out and followed Faith to a few officers standing in front of the entrance to the terminal.

Along with several hundred people.

"What the hell?" Faith muttered under her breath.

"Yeah," Michael said.

To the officers, he shouted, "Hey, what the hell is this?"

One of the officers, who wore the stripes of a sergeant on his uniform, lifted his hand and said sternly, "Sir, you need to move along."

Michael pulled his laminate and said, "Yeah, FBI numbnuts. I'm Special Agent Michael Prince, and this is my partner, Special Agent Faith Bold and our K9 unit, Turk. We're supposed to be here investigating a crime scene."

The sergeant's attitude changed immediately. His eyes widened, and his tone was much more contrite when he said, "I apologize, Special Agent. I'm Detective Sergeant Emilio Rameses, and this is officer Colton Wales. We can escort you to the scene."

"What is all this?" Faith asked. "I thought the terminal was closed."

"It was," Rameses said, "up until midnight."

"I thought it opened at six in the morning."

"It did," Rameses explained. "Today is the start of twenty-four-hour service. As you can see, it's already very popular."

"Jesus Christ," Michael muttered.

"Did you at least cordon off the scene?" Faith asked.

"I did," Rameses said, "but I'll be honest, it's likely the cordon's been removed."

"You didn't assign officers to watch the cordon?"

"I did," Rameses explained again, "but this service expansion is one of our mayor's major campaign promises, and the rail service made it clear that our investigation was not to hamper or impede service in any way."

"Glad to know they have their priorities straight," Michael said irritably.

"For what it's worth," Rameses said, "which by my estimation is about half of a crap sandwich, I'm not happy with the situation. Unfortunately, it's out of my control. I hope the cordon is still there, but my boss made it clear that if Metro Authority tells our guys to piss off, the only reason we can stop them is a crime in progress."

"Lovely," Faith said. "Well, take us there anyway. Who knows? Maybe we'll get lucky."

They were not lucky. Rameses swore under his breath as they approached the scene, and Michael could see why. Yellow police tape lay was scattered around a fifteen-foot radius of a bench currently occupied by three bored-looking individuals with the vacant expressions of night-shift workers. At the wall behind the bench stood a pair of morose-looking uniforms glaring at an imperious woman in her mid-forties flanked by two even more morose-looking security officers.

"Officers, take my partner to the scene and see if you can convince those passengers to find another bench to sit at while our K9 investigates. We've gotten lucky before. Maybe Turk's nose will pick up something."

"Where are you going?" Rameses asked.

"I'm going to talk to Little Miss Middle Manager over there."

As Michael approached the severe-looking woman flanked by bodyguards, he overheard the woman dressing down the officers. Michael was already upset after Turk's behavior toward Ellie and Faith's refusal to discuss it, so arriving at a crime scene that had been utterly ruined for political reasons left him in no mood to deal politely with the assholes responsible.

"Your superiors were told very clearly that officers were not to be present …" the woman was saying.

"Excuse me," Michael interrupted, pulling his ID from his wallet.

The manager turned an irritated glance toward Michael that vanished almost instantly behind a perfectly polite, customer-service smile. "Sir, we have an information booth right over …" Her voice trailed off when she saw Michael's ID and realized he wasn't a passenger.

"Yeah, hi," Michael said, "Special Agent Michael Prince, FBI. And you are?"

The woman drew herself up to her full height of right around five feet and looked regally at Michael. "I'm Sita Bhandari," she said, "I'm the Managing Director of the Twin Cities Terminal. I was just informing your officers—"

"Not my officers," Michael interrupted, taking a perverse delight in the rage that flashed across her face. "I'm FBI," he said, "in case you didn't hear me the first time. That means I don't care what arrangement you have with PD. You ruined my crime scene, and unless you have a damned good reason why, I'm going to make sure that every news network whose contact information I can find online is going to know your name and that it's your fault if the killer who struck yesterday kills someone else."

Sita blinked and took a step back, and Michael once more felt perverse delight at her reaction. "Officer, I—"

"Special Agent," Michael corrected.

"Special Agent," Sita began again, "I apologize for the inconvenience posed to you and your investigators. I am under instruction by my superiors to ensure our passengers have a safe, convenient, and enjoyable experience at this terminal, and that precludes roping off a section of our seating area and a concerning police presence."

"I see," Michael said, "and how do you propose to keep people safe from the murderer who killed a man and left his body sitting on the bench for a coffee cart worker to find?"

Sita met Michael's gaze and said, "I'm sure you know as well as me that appearances matter more than reality to upper management."

Michael's frustration toward Sita faded instantly when she said that. "Yeah," he said, running his hands through his hair. "Yeah, I know how that goes."

"For what it's worth," Sita said, "I am sorry for the circumstances. I would allow you to complete your investigation unfettered if the decision was mine, but …" she lifted her hands and let them drop.

"Right," Michael said. "Who specifically gave the instruction to tear down the cordon?"

"I'm not sure," Sita said. "It was sent to me as an urgent administrative memo from the Board of Directors. I don't know which of them specifically enacted the motion. Honestly, though, it wouldn't have to be a motion. Any one of the board members could have made the executive decision and sent the memo as an order from the entire board."

"Well, I'll tell you what," Michael said, pulling a business card out of his wallet. "Why don't you email me a list of the members of the board and any senior officers who would have had the authority to make this call, and if you have a card yourself, I'd like to take it. My partner and I may have more questions for you later."

"I'll give you my card," Sita said, reaching into her own wallet, "but you can find all of this information online."

"I'll still take the card," Michael said, handing her his, "and I still want that email. Also, I want access to the security footage from last night."

"I'll have the email sent to you later today," she said. "I need to be on the floor during the first few overnights in case any emergencies arise that need a manager's presence. The security footage may take a day or two longer. It's a new system, and we're still learning the basics."

"Fine," Michael said. "Whenever's convenient for you."

Sita bristled at Michael's short tone but nodded and handed him his card. She left to continue her hunt for emergencies that might need a manager's presence, and Michael turned to the two officers, who looked at him with something akin to worship.

"Notice anything unusual, officers?"

The female officer replied, "I'm afraid not. The scene was pretty well combed through by the time we got here, and we were almost immediately told to stand down."

"That's wonderful," Faith's voice interjected, full of sarcasm, "because the scene has been 'combed through' so well by now that not even Turk can get a read."

Michael turned to see Faith and Turk approaching with the two officers. "I just talked to the manager," Michael said, "Apparently, the order to clear the scene came from the Metro Authority's Board of Directors."

"I'm not surprised," Faith said. "I imagine the real order came from the mayor's office."

"Probably," Michael said. "I asked her for the names and contact info for the board of directors anyway."

"Good call," Faith said. "Detective Rameses, I'd like to talk to the officers who first responded to the call."

"Well, that would be Officer Wales," Rameses said, "and Officer Park. She's off duty tonight, but I'll let her know to contact you when she starts in the morning."

"Thank you," Faith said. "In the meantime, I'll let you wrap things up on your end. Can we borrow Officer Wales, or is he your ride?"

"I'll ride with one of the other officers. He's all yours."

CHAPTER FIVE

Officer Wales looked to be fresh out of the Academy, maybe twenty-two or twenty-three or a young-looking twenty-five at the outside. The experience, at least, was confirmed when Michael asked, "How long have you been with the force, Wales?"

Wales chuckled with just a touch of bitter humor that Faith knew would become far more than a touch with a few more years under his belt. "Just about fifteen months," he said. "That was my first dead body."

"It gets easier," Michael said with a more advanced undertone of bitter humor.

Colton nodded. "Well, you asked what happened, so from the top. Nine-one-one received a call from a very distressed Kylie Bonaparte at six minutes to two in the afternoon yesterday. Officer Park and I responded to discover the young lady in significant distress over her discovery of one Chester McIlhenny, sixty-four, who was murdered and left on the park bench sometime before the hour of six a.m. that morning. We're currently waiting on the security footage from the Metro Authority to determine the exact time he was left here."

"We'll see if we can put some pressure on them for you," Michael said.

"We'd appreciate that," Colton said. "Although at this point, it's more for you than for me."

"When you arrived at the scene," Faith said, "was the scene already contaminated?"

"Oh yeah," Colton replied. "There was a whole crowd around the body and security was having a hard enough time keeping people from touching it."

"Can you tell me the names of the security officers who responded?" Faith asked.

"I'm afraid not," Colton replied, lowering his eyes. "I—this was my first dead body, and I was focused on securing the scene. I'm afraid I didn't get any witness contact information other than Miss Bonaparte."

“Don’t beat yourself up too badly, kid,” Michael said. “The first one’s always tough. I’ll follow up with the manager to determine who was on duty that morning.”

“When the scene was secure,” Faith continued, “did you perform the initial examination of the scene?”

“No ma’am,” Wales said. “I called it in, and they instructed me to wait for CSI.”

“We’ll talk to them next,” Faith said. “Anything you noticed at all unusual?”

“Not really,” Officer Wales said, somewhat glumly. “I just called the scene in.”

“No marks, no unusual clothing.”

“Well, his entire outfit was unusual,” Colton said. “Trench coat, hat, sunglasses that looked like they came from a fifties movie.” He cocked his head and said, “Come to think of it, I did notice something unusual. His clothing looked new. Like, brand new.”

Faith exchanged a glance with Michael. If the clothing was brand new, odds were that the killer had bought them to stage McIlhenny.

“Any idea what the brands were?”

“Not a clue,” Colton replied. “I’m not exactly the most fashionable person in the world. The coroner should have all that information. I can give you the address and phone number.”

“We’ll take that,” Faith said. “Also the contact info for Miss Bonaparte.”

Colton provided them the info, and Faith thanked him. Before he left, Michael said, “Hey kid, take it from someone who knows, go get your head checked. No one likes a psych eval, but I’m telling you you’ll be better off for it.”

Faith’s lips tightened slightly at the advice, but she kept silent. Michael was only offering helpful advice to a young officer, not attacking her. Besides, she was seeing Doctor West now.

Colton nodded and said, “Will do. Thank you.”

After he left, Michael asked Faith, “You think he’ll go see a shrink?”

Faith sighed, “Probably not. He’ll talk to Rameses about it, and Rameses will probably tell him not to waste his time on that. He’ll listen to Rameses. Younger guys idolize experienced detectives.”

“Is that why you resisted for so long?”

Now, he was attacking her.

She sighed. “Do you want to fight right now, Michael?”

"No," he said. "No fighting. Sorry I brought it up."

"It's fine," Faith said. "Let's call Miss Bonaparte?"

"I don't think she's going to be awake," Michael said. "It's only three in the morning."

"I don't care what time it is," Faith said. "We don't know how fast this killer operates. She's the closest thing we have to a witness right now, and I don't feel like waiting for the information."

"All right, fair enough," Michael said. "There's no need to get pissy with me."

Faith's lips tightened again, but she let the jibe go without response. Michael dialed the number, and Faith reached down to stroke Turk behind his neck. The K9 was as irritable as the agents, growling and sniffing in circles around Faith.

"It's not your fault, boy," Faith told him. "This is just a tough crime scene. We'll find him."

"Yes, Miss Bonaparte?" Michael said. "This is Special Agent Michael Prince with the FBI. I'm calling in regard to your recent report of a murder in the Twin City Terminal yesterday afternoon. I was wondering if my partner and I could come ask you a few questions?" He paused a moment. "Yes, I understand you've already spoken with police. I'd like to ask some follow-up questions pertinent to the Bureau's investigation." Another pause. "I'd prefer to do it in person." Another pause. "Thank you, Miss Bonaparte. No, that's okay, we'll come to you. I appreciate it." He pulled a pen and notepad from his suit pocket and said, "Okay, I'm ready, go ahead." He wrote down the address then said, "Thank you. We'll be there shortly."

He hung up and turned to Faith, "You might want to take lead on this one. She seemed very wary of me."

"Works for me," Faith said. "Don't take it personally. She's probably just choked up after what she saw."

"I never take anything personally," Michael said. Seeing Faith's expression, he added, "on a case."

"Sure you don't," Faith said.

She looked around the terminal, which despite the fact that this was the witching hour was crowded with people. She could only imagine what the place was like during the morning rush. "All right," she said. "Let's head out."

Fortunately, the roads weren't nearly as crowded as the subway, at least not by urban standards. Michael estimated five minutes to make it to Miss Bonaparte's apartment. While they drove, Faith took stock of what they knew so far.

Chester McIlhenny, sixty-four, member of the jury that convicted August Hornfeldt and recommended the death penalty. Murdered via means currently unknown and staged in the Twin Cities Terminal on a bench where he was ignored for hours until a barista who had also ignored him for hours decided to check on him. Dressed in an unusual outfit purchased recently, possibly by the killer himself. Or herself. Or theirself.

God, she was tired. Maybe she could convince Miss Bonaparte to make her some coffee while they talked, she thought wryly.

"We need to look into the Hornfeldt case," she said to Michael. "See if there's a connection there."

"That's next on my list after Bonaparte and the coroner," Michael replied.

"Your list?"

Michael rolled his eyes, "*Our* list. If that's all right with you, ma'am."

Faith looked at him. "I can't tell if this is banter or if you're still angry at me."

Michael sighed, "Let's just focus on the case."

"Well, that answers that question," Faith said.

They reached Miss Bonaparte's apartment just in time for Michael to avoid responding. Miss Bonaparte lived in a working-class complex that was just this side of being a slum. The major difference Faith noted was that the complex was clean. That was about all the place had going for it. Not that it likely mattered much to a college student living on her own in the middle of the largest metropolitan area in the United States.

Kylie Bonaparte opened the door before the agents even reached her unit. "Saw you through the window," she explained. "You want to come inside?"

"If that's all right with you," Faith said.

Kylie looked at her. "You're Special Agent Prince's partner?"

"Faith Bold," Faith replied. "You can just call me Faith."

Kylie nodded. Her eyes were puffy and dark bags hung underneath them. Her skin was otherwise pale, and streaks of yesterday's makeup ran down her cheeks. She had clearly spent a sleepless night crying. No doubt this was the reason she was awake when Michael called.

Kylie looked at Turk and smiled softly. "Who's the puppy?"

"That's Turk, our K9 unit."

Kylie sighed. "Well, he was there when I arrived at work. I remember thinking that was unusual since the terminal doesn't open until six, or at least it didn't until today, but I just assumed he was one of the homeless people we get sometimes. He was dressed unusually, so I thought maybe he was a street performer."

"At what point did you suspect he might have been in trouble?"

"Um," Kylie said, "not at all, really. Not until I left and realized he was sitting in the same place for hours. It was strange, too, the way he was sitting. Honestly, I probably wouldn't have thought to check him otherwise."

"Strange?" Faith asked, her ears pricking up. "How so?"

"He was sitting kind of like this." She leaned back in her chair with one arm lifted at the elbow and bent backward at the wrist, the fingers splayed. "Kind of like he was drinking a martini or something. I remember noticing that around my lunch break, and when I left and his hand was in the same position, I—well, I guess I thought he might be dead. I wish I was wrong."

"I'm sorry you had to see that," Faith said.

Kylie offered a slight smile that disappeared almost instantly. "It makes me scared to go to work, you know? I don't know what happened with Mr. McIlhenny, but I work early in the morning. I guess I won't be alone now that the terminal's open for twenty-four hours, but still, it kind of sucks to know that stuff like this happens."

"I know," Faith said. "People can be terrible."

Kylie offered another slight, transient smile.

"When you discovered Mr. McIlhenny's true condition," Faith continued, "what happened immediately after that?"

"Immediately after? I screamed. Really loud. A bunch of people started to crowd around and freak out. Well, most of them freaked out. Some of them started taking pictures and videos and stuff. You know, the typical immature childish stuff."

"Right," Faith said. "When were the police called?"

"As soon as I stopped screaming," Kylie replied. "Maybe five minutes?"

"And how long did it take for police to respond?"

"Not long. The terminal is a high traffic area, and there are always officers around during business hours."

Faith nodded. "Did you notice anything unusual about Mr. McIlhenny other than his dress and seating position?"

She shook her head. "Not really. I mean, he was covered from head to toe, so if he was wounded or something, I wouldn't really be able to see anything."

"What about from anyone else at the terminal? Did anyone behave unusually or seem suspicious or out of the ordinary to you?"

"No, not really," she replied. "I mean, I see tons of people every day, and I see a lot of unusual things, so I wouldn't know really if people were being strange or if that's just how they always are."

"But no one especially comes to mind from yesterday?"

She shook her head. "No, not really. Sorry."

"No need to apologize," Faith said. "You've been very helpful. Is there anything else you think we need to know?"

She shook her head again.

"All right," Faith said.

She stood and reached inside her wallet for a card. "If you do think of anything else, Kylie, please let us know. Rest assured, the FBI and the police department are doing everything we can to apprehend this killer."

Kylie offered a smile that did not seem at all reassured. She took Faith's card and gave Turk a hug before walking the two agents to the door. She gave Turk another hug before they left, and Faith's heart went out to her. She was so young—too young to see things like this.

Then again, Faith was only nineteen when she was shipped to Afghanistan to see far worse things than Kylie had seen. She wondered if Kylie would recover from her trauma the way that Faith had recovered from hers.

Then she wondered if she ever did recover from the trauma of warfighting or if Trammell's attack only exacerbated a problem that existed long before she'd ever heard of the Donkey Killer. She decided to ask Doctor West about that the next time they spoke.

Michael called the coroner's office as soon as they were in the car. The office was a distance removed from the urban center, and Michael announced it would take them twenty-five minutes to reach it. Faith decided to take a nap on the way. She managed to close her eyes, but as often happened when she was working a case, her mind raced too much for her to sleep.

Why would someone kill a man, change his outfit, and stage him on a bench in a subway terminal? What message was he trying to send? Or was he just crazy?

In Faith's experience, the answer was a combination of both.

In Faith's experience, that meant this killer was incredibly dangerous.

CHAPTER SIX

The coroner's office was located in a massive precinct building that was nearly as large as the Philadelphia Field Office. Faith and Michael checked in with reception and were quickly ushered to the coroner's office.

The coroner was a stocky woman of around forty who introduced herself as Amy Ashley. "I know," she said, "two first names. My parents have a very well-developed sense of humor."

"Do you prefer Amy or Miss Ashley?" Michael asked.

"Well, aren't you polite?" Amy answered with a smile. "Amy's fine. You're here about Mr. McIlhenny?"

"Yes," Faith said. "Can we see him?"

"Follow me."

Amy led them down a flight of stairs toward the basement where the autopsy rooms and morgue were located. "Can't stand elevators," she said. "Did you ever see that horror movie where Naomi Watts is a reporter who investigates a possessed elevator?"

"Can't say I have," Michael replied.

"Well, there's a scene where a guy gets cut in half by the elevator," Amy explained. "Ever since then, I can't stand taking elevators."

"Makes sense," Faith replied.

"You'd think I wouldn't mind so much considering my job," Amy said, "but there's always a way out, you know? I'm never trapped when I'm in an autopsy room. Even the morgue has multiple exits, so there's always a way out. Anyway, here we are."

Chester McIlhenny was sixty-four years old when he died and looked it. He was not one of those older men who took care of himself well and remained hale and hearty past middle age. His skin was somehow flabby and leathery at the same time and liberally sprinkled with liver spots. He wasn't especially overweight, but what little extra weight he did carry he carried in a rotund paunch that formed an almost perfect circle between his belt and his ribcage. All in all, he looked like a man who had long since given up on his health, if he had ever tried.

Amy evidently agreed with Faith's assessment. "Not much of a looker, is he? Guess he didn't get the memo that sixty is the new forty."

"Any sign of injury?" Michael asked.

"Not that anyone would have seen," Amy said, "but I do know the cause of death."

She tilted Chester's head to the left and turned it slightly so the agents could see a tiny little prick just underneath his ear behind his jaw.

Faith's eyes widened. "Poison?"

"Yep. Specifically, phenol."

Michael whistled.

"Phenol?" Faith asked. "Like what they use for lethal injections?"

"Well, not anymore. Mostly, lethal injection is a combination of pancuronium bromide, potassium chloride, and midazolam. But yes, phenol has been used for lethal injection before. As you can see, it's very effective."

"No other signs of injury?" Faith asked.

"None," Amy said. She released his head and said, "Not even defensive wounds. Either he was asleep when the attack happened, or it happened so fast that he never even noticed it." She looked up at the agents and grinned sheepishly. "Sorry. That's your job to figure out. I'll only say that this little pinprick was the only sign of injury."

"Where might someone get phenol?" Michael asked.

"Well, if you want pure phenol, you need to get it from a chem lab. However, if you have a decently well-stocked home lab and a little know how, you can separate it from medical-grade sanitizer or sore throat spray."

"So, we're looking for a professional in the medical, chemical, or pharmaceutical fields," Faith said.

"Well, not necessarily," Amy said. "You can buy sore throat spray with phenol over the counter. All you have to do is be over twenty-one with no drug-related felonies on your record."

"Lovely," Faith said, "so our guy could literally be anyone."

"Well, in order to source enough pure phenol to kill someone by injection, he'd need to have at least a little chemistry know-how. Say, undergraduate level chem student. Think fourth year and above."

"So, likely someone with a professional background."

"That would be my guess," Amy agreed, "but then again, I'm not a detective."

"Thank you for your time, doctor," Faith said. "It goes without saying that if you find anything else, we need to be your first call."

Amy raised an eyebrow. "Problems with the police?"

"The police have problems, but not with us," Faith explained. "We're not concerned with local politics, so we have freedom to act on information and make sure it isn't buried before we can act on it."

Amy nodded knowingly. "I get that. Politicians are assholes."

"That's my experience," Faith said.

Amy looked down at their victim and said, "Funny thing. He was on the verge of congestive heart failure. Odds are, he would have been dead in six months if our killer had just left him alone."

"That would require the killer to think rationally," Faith pointed out.

"Yeah," Amy said. "I guess you're right."

"Any family?" Michael asked.

"None within three hundred miles," Amy said. "Cops can tell you more, but from what I understand, everyone has an ironclad alibi. Chester here was close to a black sheep. Not quite despised but not quite loved. No money either, so no reason for family to come pay final respects. It's sad, really. Then again, I guess he won't know the difference."

"No," Faith said. "I guess not."

They left the coroner's office and headed for their hotel. It was after five in the morning, and the first rays of dawn were creeping over the horizon, so they weren't going to get any sleep, but they could unpack and grab breakfast and coffee before they followed up on the court case Chester was assigned to.

Turk fell promptly asleep in the hotel room, and since Faith didn't want to leave him alone, they ate breakfast in the room. The breakfast was a half-step up from the typical crap served at hotels, Faith noticed. Only a half-step, though. She wondered how much of the depression law enforcement agents suffered was a result of constant exposure to bad food and even worse coffee.

"Think our killer will strike again?" Michael asked.

"Hopefully, they won't get the chance," Faith said. "But if you're asking, will they try? Yes, I think so. Distilling a medical-grade anesthetic and injecting someone in the neck then dressing him in comic book detective clothes and staging him on a bench in the second-busiest subway terminal in the largest city in America is about as serial killer as you can get."

"He could have just had something against Chester personally."

"Possibly," Faith said, "but I doubt it. Either way, we should assume that he'll strike again."

"Wonderful," Michael said. "I just love seeing killers stack bodies."

"It's the job we chose," Faith said.

"Faith, sometimes you annoy me more than anyone else I've ever met."

"You constantly annoy me more than anyone I've ever met," Faith retorted. "So, I'm thinking we meet with the judge presiding over the Hornfeldt case and go from there."

"Way ahead of you," Michael said. "Justice Andrea Mullens. Her chambers open at seven a.m. I took the liberty of calling her secretary and getting us an appointment first thing."

"How did you get a hold of her secretary?" Faith asked.

"Well, it's the court secretary," Michael said, "the overnight receptionist."

"I'm impressed anyway," Faith said.

"Well, thank you," Michael said. "So, when are we going to talk about why you don't like Ellie?"

Faith sighed. "We're not going to talk about it, Michael. I've already told you it's not my business. I don't think she's dangerous enough that I have to intervene to save your life. In fact, I don't dislike her. I know you're pissed about Turk's behavior, and I really do feel bad about that, but at the end of the day, Michael, she's your girlfriend, and even if she were a raging bitch, it's not my place to say anything. So, can we just drop it?"

"Sure," Michael said, "until the case is over. I do want an answer from you, though."

"Well," Faith said, standing and drinking the last of her coffee, "we're on the case now, so let's just leave that talk for later."

"All right," Michael said. "Where are you going though? It's only six o'clock. We don't need to leave for another forty minutes."

"I'm going to shower," she said. "Would you like to join me?"

Michael stared at her in shock, and she rolled her eyes. "Joking, Michael. That was a joke."

"I can't tell with you anymore," he said.

Faith lingered in the shower, allowing the warm water to ease the tension in her body. Michael was going to be testy for the entire case, and Faith wasn't looking forward to it. Their relationship had grown more and more strained over the past several months, and Ellie's arrival had only further complicated things.

What could she do, though? *Hey, Michael, I think your girlfriend is still fucking her ex-husband. Hey, Michael, I don't think Ellie loves or even likes you that much. Hey, Michael, I'm not sure why, but Ellie's using you.*

Yeah, she could just hear that conversation.

She finished her shower and toweled off, then headed to the room to grab her bag. Michael glanced at her, but his glance didn't linger. She wondered why she noticed that.

God, she couldn't wait to get home.

They drove in silence to the courthouse until they parked. Before Faith could exit, Michael said, "I'm sorry, Faith. I know I'm allowing personal issues to interfere with my job. It threw me for a loop to see Turk behave that way with Ellie, and I know you don't—well, it doesn't matter. I'll forget about all of that until the job is done, okay? Case first, everything else second."

"I appreciate that, Michael," Faith said.

They said nothing else on the subject, but the tension was somewhat eased between them as they walked inside. The officer manning the metal detector insisted that they surrender their weapons, not relenting until his supervisor came over and waved the two agents through.

"Here's hoping our judge is more pleasant than Officer Fife over there," Michael said.

Justice Andrea Mullens was a plain-looking woman of around fifty with dyed, shoulder-length, brown hair and an expression that was the perfect balance between regal, contemptuous, bored, and irritable. She looked born to be a judge and wore her robes well.

"I understand you're investigating the murder of Chester McIlhenny," she told the agents, "and that you believe the perpetrator is a member of August Hornfeldt's defense?"

"The first part is true," Faith said. "The second part is getting ahead of ourselves. What we want to know is if anyone threatened any of the jurors or Chester in particular or expressed a wish that they should suffer harm?"

"Yes," the judge said. "One person did. Richard Hornfeldt."

The last name caught Faith's attention. She leaned forward and said, "Any relation to August Hornfeldt?"

"Yes, his son," Mullens confirmed. "He vowed that the jurors who sentenced his father to death would, I believe he said, 'get what's coming to them.'"

Faith and Michael exchanged a glance. "Did anyone else make a threat or seem threatening?"

"No," Andrea said. "The majority of people supported the death penalty. Even those who didn't felt no grief at the sentence. In fact, I believe Mr. Hornfeldt—Richard, that is—was the only one angered by my judgment."

"May I ask why you didn't pass this information along to the police when you heard of Mr. McIlhenny's death?"

"To be honest, Miss Bold, I assumed the information was already publicly available. Typically, when the adult children of serial killers threaten to harm or kill others, it becomes a sensation."

"Fair enough," Faith said. "In general, how did people feel about Mr. McIlhenny?"

"In general? They felt nothing. They felt the same as anyone feels about anyone they don't know well. From what I understand, he was a capable foreman but rather quiet and more disposed to let others argue than to take an active role himself."

"So, he was the foreman of the jury," Michael said.

"Yes," Andrea confirmed, "though that wouldn't grant him any special power or influence over the judgment."

"Still," Michael said, "he was the one who announced the verdict. That might be enough to inspire Ricky-boy to target him as his father's murderer."

"Perhaps," Andrea said. "Now, if there's nothing else, I have a very full docket today, and I would like to have time to prepare."

"Of course, your honor," Faith said, standing. "Thank you for your time."

Back in the car, they looked up Hornfeldt's address. He lived in a middle-class neighborhood just outside the city, about a fifteen-minute drive from the courthouse.

"Think he'll be home?" Faith asked.

"Eight in the morning on a workday? I doubt it, but it's worth a shot. You never know these days what with virtual offices and scattered workweeks."

"Well, fingers crossed," Faith said. "Do you have a workplace if the home doesn't pan out?"

"Dave's Sporting Goods." Michael said. "Not sure what location yet."

Faith gave him a thumbs up. "All right then," she said. "Let's go talk to him."

***

They reached Hornfeldt's home at eight o'clock exactly. Turk was alert as they approached the house but not particularly antsy or excitable. That didn't necessarily mean Hornfeldt wasn't the killer, especially since Turk hadn't picked up a scent at the crime scene, but it wasn't a great sign of guilt, either.

They knocked on the door and received no response, which wasn't surprising. Hornfeldt's car wasn't in the driveway. He could have parked in his garage, but there were no lights on in the house either, and when Faith pressed her ear to the door, she could hear no sounds coming from inside. No TV drone, no footsteps, no running water.

"Odds are he's not home," Faith said. "What do you think? Do we break in and search? Probable cause because of the threat?"

"I think that flies," Michael said. "Let's just try not to make a mess."

Faith knelt in front of the door and used her bobby pin to jig the tumbler. She just managed to get the door unlocked when she heard a voice behind them.

"Hey! What are you two doing? I'm calling the police!"

She stood and turned while Michael lifted his ID toward a balding man in a wifebeater who leaned out of the driver's window of an ostentatiously oversized diesel pickup and glared at the two agents. "Special Agent Michael Prince, FBI. This is my partner, Special Agent Faith Bold and our K9 unit, Turk. We're here on official FBI business."

"You have a badge number?" the man challenged.

"F65837," Michael said, "but you'll want to contact the Bureau to verify that not the police."

"What are you doing here?" the man demanded.

Faith and Michael started toward the truck. When they were close enough not to shout, Michael asked, "Are you the neighbor?"

"Lester Caine," the man said. "What's Richard in trouble for? This doesn't have to do with his old man, does it?"

"Where is Mr. Hornfeldt?" Faith asked.

"He's in Buffalo for his kid's baseball game," Lester said. "Won't be back until late."

"The game was today?"

"Last night," Lester said.

"When did Mr. Hornfeldt leave for the game?" Michael asked.

"Not sure," Lester said. "I haven't seen his car since Friday. He usually parks in the driveway, but he could've parked in his garage. I'm out most days from five in the morning until five at night, so I might have missed him."

"How is Mr. Hornfeldt?" Faith asked. "As a neighbor, I mean?"

"He's wonderful," Lester replied. "Always there to lend a hand when I or someone else here needs it. It was terrible about his father. I can't believe a monster like that raised a class act like Richard." He shook his head. "I feel even worse for his boy."

"His boy?"

"Yeah, his son, Daniel. Good kid, nine or ten."

"That the baseball player?" Michael asked.

"Yeah, shortstop. Great arm. Could have been a pitcher, but he hits for contact sweeter than Stan Musial. My nephew plays in the same league. Different team, though. They're from Queens. My sister-in-law is."

"After his father was indicted," Faith asked, "did you notice a change in Mr. Hornfeldt's behavior?"

"Well, he was angry to all hell," Lester said. "Kept calling the jurors assholes and talking about what he'd do if he got them alone. I chalked it up to typical distress over his father getting the death penalty. Wait, he didn't actually kill one of the jurors, did he?"

"I'm afraid I can't comment about an active investigation," Michael said. "Can you confirm Mr. Hornfeldt's whereabouts two nights ago?"

Lester shook his head. "I can tell you I didn't see his car, but like I said, sometimes he parks in the garage. Look, Richard's a good guy. We've been friends for years. I know you guys have to follow up, but I'll vouch for Richard. He's not the killing type."

"Right," Michael said. "Well, thank you, Mr. Caine. If you think of anything else, please give us a call."

He handed Caine his card, and the neighbor drove off. He parked three houses down from Hornfeldt's residence and gave the agents a friendly wave as he walked inside.

Faith and Michael glanced at each other. "Do you still want to search his place?" Michael asked.

"We can table that for now," Faith said. "Buffalo is six-and-a-half hours away from New York City, figure eight with a stop for the kids to use the restroom and get some gas and lunch. We'll come back then. In the meantime, we can follow up with the other jurors and the Metro Authority board. It's probably not going to yield anything helpful, but I've been wrong about that before, and we don't have any other leads."

“We’re sure Hornfeldt didn’t do a runner?” Michael asked. “You want to put out an APB on the vehicle?”

“Good idea,” Faith said.

Michael called for the APB while Faith knelt next to Turk. “What do you think, boy?” she asked. “Do you think he’s the bad guy?”

Turk offered a noncommittal head toss, then resumed his watch on a squirrel who eyed him warily from the branches of an oak tree that stood on the sidewalk next to Hornfeldt’s house.

“Yeah, I don’t know either,” she said.

All signs pointed to Hornfeldt being the prime suspect, but Faith already felt unsure about that. His behavior indicated rage not cold calculation. If McIlhenny had been bludgeoned to death, Faith would feel much more strongly that Hornfeldt was responsible, but to poison him and then stage him somewhere public where he could easily be found? It didn’t make sense.

Then again, serial killers didn’t make sense, and in Hornfeldt’s case, at least, killing ran in the family.

CHAPTER SEVEN

He almost laughed but stopped himself. If he had, then the cops in the terminal might have noticed him laughing at their confusion and wondered what he thought was so funny. He almost laughed again thinking how silly it would be if he were caught because he found the police department's incompetence funny.

The FBI was far less incompetent than the NYPD, at least according to his limited research on the topic, but he wasn't worried about them. Law enforcement operated by finding things that stood out, things that shouldn't be where or what they were.

He was invisible. Not the noticeable kind of invisible where something that clearly should be there wasn't there, but the kind of invisible that looked exactly as it should and wasn't at all interesting.

He wondered what his name would be when he killed enough that people started to sensationalize his killings. He supposed they could call him the Chameleon because he was invisible and disguised his victims. That would fit, he supposed, if one considered that his victims were dressed to be noticeably unnoticeable. He himself, however, wasn't a chameleon, shifting colors but not shape to confuse poor-sighted predators.

He fancied himself more of a moth, specifically the peppered moth. The peppered moth didn't change color. It was born with the perfect dull, mottled pattern of gray, white, and brown necessary to hide among the bark of trees located in industrial urban centers. It's coloration perfectly matched the color of soot and bark and did so without resorting to trickery.

He was particularly proud of himself for making his victim just noticeable enough. It was a hard balance to strike, hiding him in plain sight but making him just obvious enough that anyone paying attention should have picked up on the fact that something was amiss.

Anyone paying attention. That was the key. People had to pay attention, but they didn't. They never did. Unless it impacted them directly, people very easily blinded themselves to the plight of … well, pretty much everyone.

Like this homeless woman begging for change in the terminal. He watched in disgust and anger as no fewer than twenty people passed her by without so much as a glance.

One in particular grabbed his attention, a sharply dressed, up-and-coming Wall Streeter who didn't ignore the homeless woman but glanced at her with naked contempt, as though it offended him that she would dare to suffer misfortune in his vicinity.

He recognized that young man, oh yes, he did. That young man, who when he purchased his newspaper every morning couldn't be bothered to thank the shopkeeper. That young man who spent most of his time on his phone loudly bragging about his success in business and shoving past anyone he felt was traveling slower than they should.

This young man wasn't just indifferent, but he was also callous. He didn't consider the thoughts or feelings of others, except perhaps when it suited his financial ambitions.

Well, he would learn. He would see the errors of his ways. Or rather, others would and through his example, they would think long and hard about showing the same indifference.

He checked his watch, said goodbye to his coworkers, and headed for home. He passed the Wall Streeter without so much as a glance. His time would come soon enough.

CHAPTER EIGHT

"So, the Metro Authority is a bunch of dicks as we expected them to be," Michael said, "but no sign they're the killers, and anyway, they have solid alibis. They made a point of telling me they'd include my name in their complaint to the Bureau. I really hope they get the Boss's number."

Faith and Michael were eating dinner at the hotel. The sky was just starting to darken as the sun touched the western horizon. Faith could tell from Michael's expression that his day had been just as fruitless as hers.

"You know the Boss will rip you a new one for getting him involved with politics," she said.

"Yeah, but I can handle that," Michael said. "These guys have no idea what they're getting into."

Faith chuckled briefly and said, "Well, I can't offer much more help. The other jurors are all frightened, but they all had good alibis too. None of them seemed to think much of Chester either way, positive or negative. They seemed to like that he was uninvolved and wanted to go with the flow."

"Go with the flow," Michael said. "Gotta love jury by your peers."

Faith shrugged. "I'm staying away from that conversation," she said. "Any luck on the bulletin?"

As if on cue, Michael's phone rang. He answered and, after a moment, smiled. "Thank you, Officer. If you can keep him there until we arrive, that would be great. Shouldn't take more than twenty minutes."

"They got him here? In the city?" Faith asked.

"Yep. He's at a park about five minutes from his house."

"His kid's there?"

"Yep. Think we should tell the officer to take him somewhere?"

"Not yet. After Turk gets a good read on him, we can use him to occupy the son and talk to Mr. Hornfeldt in private."

"Good idea," Michael said.

They reached the park as promised twenty minutes after Michael hang up. Richard Hornfeldt stood with his arms crossed, arguing with the two officers who had stopped him. His son hovered just behind him, his eyes wide as saucers.

When he saw the dog approaching, the son shrank back until Turk offered a friendly bark and then trotted up to him, tail wagging. Richard stepped quickly in front of his son, but Turk, rather than reacting aggressively, just looked at him, bewildered. It seemed Turk didn't sense a threat from him.

"We'll take it from here, officers," Faith said. "Thank you."

The officers nodded and the older of the two asked, "You want us to stick around, just in case?"

"Actually, now that you mention it," Faith said, "if you wouldn't mind watching my dog while I talk to Mr. Hornfeldt. I was thinking this handsome, young man here might want to play with him while we ask his dad a few questions."

The boy's eyes popped open, and he looked pleadingly at his father.

"What's this about?" Richard asked irritably.

"I think it's in everyone's best interests if we speak privately, Mr. Hornfeldt," Michael said.

Richard frowned but allowed his son to leave with Turk. The officers exchanged a glance, clearly unhappy with being saddled with babysitting duty, but they complied without protest.

When Hornfeldt's son was out of earshot, Faith and Michael started questioning him.

"Mr. Hornfeldt, can you tell us your whereabouts two nights ago?" Faith asked.

"Two nights ago? I was in Buffalo. We got in around eight-thirty."

"Do you have anyone who can verify that?"

"Um, I mean, you can call the hotel. They can verify that my son and I checked in. I'm sure they have security cameras too."

"Which hotel is that?"

"Sunrise Inn. You need the number?"

"This the one?" Michael said, holding his phone up.

"Yeah, that's it. Comfortable rooms and not too pricey either."

"If I'm ever in Buffalo, I'll keep it in mind."

"Mr. Hornfeldt, what were your thoughts when you heard about Mr. McIlhenny's death?" Faith asked.

"Who?"

Faith and Michael shared a glance.

"Mr. Chester McIlhenny," Faith said.

Hornfeldt regarded them with a blank stare that appeared as genuine as any look of confusion Faith had ever seen. Faith sighed and added, "He was the foreman of the jury during your father's trial."

"Oh." His face darkened. "I wasn't aware he'd passed."

"You weren't aware that someone had murdered him and left his body on a bench in the Twin Cities Terminal?" Michael said.

"Jesus," Richard said. "God. No, I wasn't aware. Is that what this is about? Someone killed a juror on my father's trial, and you assumed it was me?"

"You have to admit, you're pretty high on the suspect list," Michael said.

"Why? Because my father's a murderer, I must be too?"

He glared at the two agents, until Faith said, "You also threatened the jurors."

Then his anger was replaced by shock. "Threatened them? I never threatened them!"

"You never said that the jurors were going to get what's coming to them?"

His eyes widened in realization. His shoulders slumped, and he said in a defeated tone. "Oh. That. Well, yes, I said that. I was angry, you know. I mean …" he lifted his hands and let them drop, "I … yeah, when I heard my father was being sentenced to death, I got angry. I went to a bar, got drunk, and said some stupid shit. Then I went home and thought better of it. I was never going to do anything about it."

"We'll follow up on that alibi," Faith said.

"And when you do, you'll determine I'm not your guy," Hornfeldt said, getting heated again.

"May I ask why you're so upset, Mr. Hornfeldt?" Michael prodded.

Hornfeldt stared at him like he'd sprouted a leg from his forehead. "Why am I *upset?* Why the hell do you think?"

"Please answer the question, Mr. Hornfeldt," Michael responded calmly.

Hornfeldt laughed bitterly. "Let's see. Why am I upset? Well, for starters, my father, who I've idolized from birth and who has been nothing but a saint to Danny and a rock for me when my wife passed away, was just revealed to be a serial killer. Here's a fun fact: he kept the bodies in his freezer."

Faith raised an eyebrow.

"Yeah, he had a big, chest freezer in his garage. He used to store meat there. Well, turns out, some of the meat he stored was Soylent

Green if you catch my drift. That means when I had Danny over there, he could have walked into the garage and seen a dead body chopped up and butchered like a fucking pig!"

The officers watching Turk and Danny glanced their direction. Hornfeldt sighed and lowered his voice.

"So yeah, I've been dealing with that. It's hard enough that I have to pretend I believe in Heaven so Danny can believe his mom is watching over him. Now I have to deal with the fact that all the kids at his school call him Grandson of Sam because his grandfather is a murderer. You know his friends don't talk to him anymore? Their parents don't want them around him. Genetics, you know." His lip curled in contempt as he said that.

"I'm sorry to hear that, Mr. Hornfeldt," Faith said.

"Are you?" Hornfeldt replied. "Three minutes ago, I was the top suspect in this McIlhenny murder because of my last name."

"You were our number one suspect because of your threatening comments toward the jurors, Mr. Hornfeldt," Michael reminded him.

"Right," Hornfeldt said, rubbing his eyes. "Right. Well, call the hotel. I wasn't here. And for what it's worth, I'm sorry he died. McIlhenny. I don't hate the jury anymore. They did what they had to do. I just …"

He looked over at his son, who played and laughed with Turk a few dozen yards away. "I should get him a dog," he said absently. "Yeah. I'll look into that."

"Everyone should have a dog," Faith agreed. "Do you have any idea who might want to hurt the jurors on your father's case? Besides yourself."

"I already told you; I don't want to hurt them," Hornfeldt said, growing heated again. "I got angry one night when I was drunk, that's it. While we're on the subject, how do you know this has anything to do with the trial?"

"Well, if you're alibi checks out—"

"When it checks out."

"—then we'll consider it might not be connected. At the moment, that's the only motive we can think of. If you have a different idea …"

Hornfeldt chuckled bitterly. "You know I talked to my father, the day before I took Danny to Buffalo for the game. I asked him why he chose the victims that he did? Why did he go after an old woman, a bum, a college student, and two dockworkers? You know what he said to me? He said he would look up a random number on his phone and count the people he saw until it landed on that number. He would skip family and close friends that he absolutely wanted to keep alive, but other than that, it was just luck of the draw."

"People don't kill people for a reason, Special Agent. Maybe they think they do, but they don't. If they kill people, it's for one reason, the same reason my father gave. Power. That's what it boils down to. Either they don't have power in their lives, and they substitute murder for that feeling, or they're just sick weirdos like my father who get a kick out of knowing they can kill people. It's never about anything other than that."

Faith and Michael remained silent for a while. Finally, Faith sighed and said, "Wait one moment."

She dialed the Sunrise Inn in Buffalo. The concierge verified that a Mr. Richard Hornfeldt had checked in at 8:27 in the evening two nights ago and remained in his room with his son until nine in the morning, hours after Mr. McIlhenny's body had been left at the Twin Cities Terminal four hundred miles away.

"Happy now?" Hornfeldt said when Faith hung up.

"You're free to go, Mr. Hornfeldt," Faith said. "Thank you for your time."

She called Turk over to them. Danny protested and wrapped Turk in a bear hug, but with gentle coaxing from his father, he dejectedly allowed Turk to return to the agents.

"Get him a dog," Faith said to Hornfeldt. "It'll help Danny." She met his eyes. "Not just Danny."

Hornfeldt nodded. "I will. Good night, Special Agent."

***

That night, Faith couldn't sleep. She kept playing Hornfeldt's words over and over in her mind. *Either they don't have power in their lives, and they substitute murder for that feeling, or they're just sick weirdos like my father who get a kick out of knowing they can kill people.*

Trammell had overpowered her. He had overpowered a lot of people. He had overpowered Special Agent Jack Preston. He had overpowered Turk as well. He certainly seemed to enjoy having power over people.

She thought about her most recent session with Doctor West. She had admitted that the worst part of her ordeal was not having control

"Is he friendly?"

"He is if you're a friend."

Michael's lips thinned at that.

Kylie nodded and said, "Well, come on inside."

She led them into an apartment that was as sparsely appointed on the inside as it was on the outside, save for a massive flatscreen TV that dominated an entire wall of the living room.

"Coffee?" she asked.

"Sure," Faith said. "Thank you."

Kylie looked at Michael, and he nodded. Kylie walked to the kitchen and fetched two mugs. Hers was already on the table. "Pot's fresh," she said. "Good stuff too. Our boss splurges on that heirloom stuff from South America. I've gotten so addicted I can't handle the chain stuff anymore."

"I'm sure it's wonderful," Faith said.

"Lucky me," Kylie replied tonelessly.

She returned with the mugs and sat down. Faith took a satisfying gulp of her coffee and sighed with pleasure and relief. "Miss Bonaparte," she began.

"Kylie's fine."

"Kylie," Faith said with a smile, "can you tell us what happened yesterday? From your point of view?"

Kylie took a sip of her own coffee, then sighed. "I started work at six that morning, which means I arrived at fifteen 'til to set up. I'm the opener, so I have to start the first batch of coffee and warm up the espresso machine, count the till, and all of that stuff."

"Do you like your job?" Faith asked.

Kylie nodded. "I do, actually. Most days, anyway. It's not too hard, and I don't have a boss breathing down my neck. It's busy as hell, but I don't mind that."

Faith asked a few other conversational questions to calm Kylie down before getting to the meat of things. The calmer Kylie was, the easier it would be for her to focus on what she witnessed and possibly remember details she would forget otherwise.

Turk was a great help in calming her down as well. As he had with so many witnesses, he immediately comforted Kylie, sitting next to her and resting his head on her lap for her to stroke.

"When did you notice Mr. McIlhenny?" Faith asked.

"Is that the … the …"

"The victim, yes," Faith said.

over the situation. Well, control was just a synonym of power. She felt powerless. Trammell had stolen that power from her, and she still hadn't gotten it back.

She rolled out of bed and opened her laptop. Michael rolled over and grumbled something but fell back to sleep almost immediately. Faith turned the brightness down on her screen to keep from waking him again and logged into the FBI server.

She searched for the Donkey Killer copycat. The search came back with a message that said, *RESTRICTED ACCESS. YOU ARE NOT AUTHORIZED TO VIEW THIS FILE.* She frowned and searched for the Copycat Killer. Hundreds of entries surfaced, so she filtered by date and sorted them by most recent. Only three cases popped up in the past year, and none of them were related to the Donkey Killer.

She searched for Jethro Trammell and got the original Donkey Killer case. Ditto the Donkey Killer search. She tried Jethro Trammell copycat and got nothing. Growing irritated, she searched Jared Greenwood, then searched for the name of the three most recent victims.

Nothing.

She took a breath and released it slowly. Special agents weren't just locked out of files. If she was denied access to the copycat killer case, it was because someone had blocked her. Could Clark have blocked her? She knew that field agents could choose to restrict access to cases they worked on, but she couldn't remember if they could do that by themselves or if they needed authorization from their SAC.

Well, the Boss couldn't know that Faith was digging, because if he did, then he'd have called her and chewed her out already. More likely, he would have hauled her ass back to Philadelphia and taken her badge and gun pending a clear psych eval.

So, Clark had figured out another way to block her. Or maybe he didn't need permission after all. Either way, she couldn't get in.

She sighed and slammed her laptop closed. Turk sat bolt upright, ears pricked. Michael rolled over and said, "Faith? What is it?"

"Nothing," she said. "Sorry. I almost dropped my laptop. I had to catch it."

Michael sighed. "Jesus, Faith. I'm trying to sleep."

"Sorry," she said.

"What were you looking at anyway?"

"Nothing," she said, setting her laptop on the nightstand and settling under the covers. "Good night, Michael."

"Yeah. Night."

Faith closed her eyes and, to her surprise, was able to sleep. This time, her nightmares weren't of being tied to a chair and tortured by Trammell, but of Trammell and August Hornfeldt admiring her while she sat on a bench wearing a trench coat and fedora, palm upraised, and eyes covered with dark sunglasses.

"She's purty, ain't she?" Trammell asked Hornfeldt.

"Almost good enough to eat," Hornfeldt replied. He smiled broadly, his teeth white and gleaming like piano keys in the shadow of the sunglasses.

Faith tried to move, but she couldn't. She wasn't bound, but her body refused to respond to her commands.

"What are you doing?" Trammell asked with a laugh.

"She's trying to move," Hornfeldt explained, "but she can't. She doesn't have the power."

He pulled a wicked-looking stun gun from his pocket and pressed the button. A jet of blue-white plasma crossed the distance between the two spikes of the gun with an audible whine.

Faith watched unmoving while Hornfeldt tested the gun a few more times.

Suddenly, the lights came on, and they were surrounded by people moving rapidly through the terminal. Faith tried to scream for help, but she couldn't. Her voice was as paralyzed as the rest of her.

"Oh, don't worry about them," Hornfeldt said, "they won't interrupt us."

Trammell laughed and leaned forward until Faith could smell his sour breath. "Let's see how you fry, little girl."

Hornfeldt approached, wearing a distended grin. He lifted the stun gun and with a hiss, jabbed it into Faith's shoulder. Excruciating pain flooded her, but paralyzed as she was, she was unable to scream, unable to react at all.

Trammell laughed while Hornfeldt shocked her over and over. The crowd thronged around them, but no one stopped to help. No one even glanced their way.

CHAPTER NINE

A loud bark woke Faith from her nightmare. She sat straight up, gasping. Next to the bed, Turk barked again, looking at her with the typical plaintive anxiety he always displayed when Faith had a nightmare.

"Faith?" Michael said. "You okay?"

Faith turned to Michael and sighed. "Yes. Sorry. Just a nightmare."

"Still having trouble with those, huh?" he asked gently.

His smile was filled with nothing other than concern and compassion, but Faith wasn't in a mood for compassion at the moment. She rolled out of bed and started putting her shoes on. "I'm fine," she said. "I'll get us breakfast."

"You still seeing Doctor West?" he asked.

She sat up and sighed heavily. "Well, I can't see him right now, Michael, considering we're on a case, but yes, I'm still seeing the therapist that our fine leader has ordered me to see."

"Okay, okay," Michael said, "I'm sorry. I just—"

"I know. You're worried about me. I appreciate it, but I'm fine. I'm okay. It wasn't the same nightmare anyway."

"What nightmare was it?"

Faith stood and said, "I don't want to talk about it. I'm going to go get breakfast for us and then we can talk about the case. I'd appreciate it if we kept our conversation professional for now."

Michael blinked, clearly hurt, and Faith sighed. "Look, I'm sorry. I just ..."

"I get it," Michael said. "Things are weird after Turk and Ellie, and you don't want to talk about it. Things are weird now that you're seeing a psychologist, and you don't want to talk about that. I'm your ex-boyfriend, and you're not sure how far you and David are going to go, and you don't want to talk about that. You want me to be your partner, but you're no longer sure if you want me to be your friend."

"Yeah, good idea, Michael," Faith said. "Make this about you."

She stormed outside and took a deep breath of the fresh air. It calmed her but didn't take away her anger.

She understood why he was upset, but she just couldn't handle feeling responsible for his emotions right now. I mean, God, it wasn't like she sicced Turk on Ellie. As far as Doctor West and David went, that was her business. Her mental health wasn't something she cared to share with Michael, and just because Michael liked to share every single facet of his newfound love didn't mean she needed to tell him about her relationship with David.

She returned with the coffee and breakfast and when Michael started to apologize, she said, "It's fine, Michael, just drop it. We have a case to solve, let's focus on that."

"Okay," Michael said, "but we do need to talk about this."

"Why, Michael?" she said, throwing her hands up in frustration. "Why do we need to talk about it? Why must we fixate on everything negative in our personal lives? Why can't we just leave our personal lives for when we're home off duty minding our *own* business? I want to be your friend, Michael, but I don't want to be your damned wife. I don't want to talk to you about my nightmares or my therapy, and I don't want to have a long discussion about your relationship with Ellie. You're dating her, not me. You love her, I don't have to. It's that simple. Now can we focus on the case, please?"

"I already said we can," Michael said, "but when this case is solved, we're picking this discussion up where we left off."

"Noted, Michael," Faith said, rubbing the bridge of her nose. "I'll look forward to our next argument. Right now, though—"

"Right, the case," he said. "So, where do we look next? I think we can safely say that the Hornfeldt case isn't related to McIlhenny's death."

"I think it's too early to say that," Faith said, relaxing. "It's true that Richard Hornfeldt isn't involved, but the fact that none of the other jurors have been targeted yet doesn't mean they won't be. Even if they aren't, McIlhenny was the foreman of the case. Our killer may have believed he would only get one chance at revenge, and McIlhenny would have been his number one target."

"Still," Michael said, "I think we should expand our horizons and see if we can find any other leads."

"I agree," Faith said. "I just don't want to dismiss the connection prematurely."

"Fair enough," Michael said. "In the meantime, I think it will be useful for us to talk to his family and friends and see if there might be another reason someone would want him dead."

"Does he have friends and family? The coroner said they didn't want anything to do with him."

"His family is estranged, but that doesn't mean they had no contact with him, just that the contact wasn't positive."

"I'm not sure I agree with that definition," Faith said, "but I'll bite. Do we know who his living relatives are?"

"I'll look him up," Michael said. "The IRS will have his info."

Faith fed Turk while Michael searched for info. Turk nudged her and met her eyes with a sympathetic stare. She smiled at him and scratched him under his chin. "I'm all right, buddy," she said. "Just another nightmare."

He nudged her again then began to eat.

"Got him," Michael said. "Chester McIlhenny, born December 17, 1958, deceased March 13, 2023. Three children, Brandon, thirty-four, David, twenty-nine, and Elizabeth, twenty-three. Wife, Norma, sixty-one, married 1979, divorced 1993. She died of cancer eight years ago, and by all accounts, his children have had no contact with him since then."

"You found all that from the IRS?" Faith asked.

"Not all of it, no. I looked into his phone and email records. Seventy instances of contact with the aforementioned between January and August 2015 when Norma died. Three since then."

"Damn," Faith said, "looks like they blamed him for their mother's death."

"Or for the separation. It's possible Norma was the one who encouraged contact with their father and when she died, the kids finally disconnected from them."

"Let's see if we can talk to the kids," Faith said, "and get the straight story from them."

"Good idea," Michael said. "I'll send you the contact info and you can get started on that. In the meantime, I'll talk to his coworkers. Looks like he worked for Anderson Lumber as a comptroller for their Northeastern office. He was eight months away from retiring with a full pension. Maybe someone didn't want him to reap the fruits of his labor."

"Works for me," Faith said, "Send it over, and I'll—"

Faith's phone buzzed, interrupting her. She checked the caller ID and frowned. "It's an NYPD number," she said.

Michael's lips thinned into a grim stare as Faith answered. He must have known already what the call was.

"Bold? It's Rameses. Is Prince with you?"

"He's here," Faith said. "Go ahead, Rameses."

"We have another body," he said. "Same place."

Faith sighed. "Okay. We're on our way."

"Make it quick," Rameses said. "We're having a hell of a time keeping the vultures away."

"You keep them away however you have to," Faith said. "If the Metro Authority gets in your way, blame it on the FBI. We'll see you soon."

"Terminal Security is helping us keep the crowds at bay," Rameses said. "Looks like they changed their tune."

"Wonderful," Faith said. "Thank God for small blessings. We'll be there in twenty minutes."

She hung up and met Michael's eyes.

"Well," Michael said glumly, "I guess we're looking at a serial killer after all."

"Not yet," Faith said. "A killer needs three victims to be a serial killer. We've only got two. Let's stop him before he gets to three."

Michael nodded. He heaved a sigh and stood. "Best job in the universe, am I right?"

"Oh yeah," Faith said, "it's killer."

CHAPTER TEN

This wasn't the plan. Not at all.

He couldn't understand it. He was so careful this time. He was worried, of course, that with the terminal opened twenty-four hours, he might be caught staging the body, but it had proven very straightforward to stage the body in a little-trafficked corner near the bench where he had placed the first body. Like last time, this one was dressed in an outfit that was mildly attention-seeking but not so strange that it would draw the eye instinctively. He was staged differently, too, leaning against the wall with his hands in his pockets and his head slumped forward. He was supposed to look asleep.

Evidently, he looked a little worse than asleep because it was less than an hour later when a passenger did a double take after passing him and screamed. It took nearly all of his willpower to keep from reacting in anger when he heard the scream.

He hoped to see the crowd pass them by. Hoped to watch them ignore this victim as they ignored the last one.

What had happened differently? Why were the indifferent masses suddenly so concerned?

He pondered this and realized his mistake as soon as the police arrived.

The crowd, which up until then had avoided the body like the plague, suddenly crowded around the scene, pushing against the officers and fighting for a glimpse at the body. His lip curled up in contempt as he watched them. They were like vultures, greedily circling a body as though attempting to feed on the corpse.

Well, of course, they were curious now. They were safe. They no longer feared death. With the agents of the law around, the killer lurking nearby could no longer harm them.

Not that they knew the killer really was lurking nearby. It must be a sixth sense left over from the time when humans were nothing more than apes cowering in corners from predators. They recoiled in fear, but once the danger had passed, another instinct took over, and they stared in fascination at the specter of the end that would one day take them all.

They were worse than indifferent. They were entertained by death.

He shook his head in disgust. His victims deserved to be ignored, to be treated as indifferently as they treated others in life, not to be examined and admired, even for so selfish and horrible a reason as this.

He would have to think of something else next time. He would have to figure out a way to show people exactly how oblivious everyone was to the world around them.

This … this was just a fluke. He had struck too soon and in the same spot. This was an aberration, nothing more. He was still right about people, and he would still show them.

He would show them all that he was right.

CHAPTER ELEVEN

"Jesus," Michael said, "Talk about the opposite of the last case."

"Well, we weren't here last time," Faith said. "For all we know, there was a crowd around the body the last time too. Kylie Bonaparte did say that people were taking selfies with McIlhenny."

"Yeah, but this is more like … hell, I don't know what it's like."

A crowd of hundreds mobbed a corridor leading to an employees only area of the terminal. A group of security and police officers stood in a semicircle, fending off the more adventurous civilians who tried to rush past the blockade for a peek at the body. At the head of the cordon stood Rameses, his face screwed up in anger and disgust, and Wales, his face white with fear.

Faith led Turk to the cordon, Michael following close behind. When she reached the officers, she spun around and called loudly. "This is an official crime scene! Everyone back off, or I'll set my K9 unit on you!"

As if he understood Faith's command, Turk growled menacingly. The crowd retreated several dozen yards and while they didn't dissipate, they didn't approach any more closely.

"Thank you for that," Rameses said. "I thought they were going to get past us for sure."

"Five more minutes and they would have," Faith said. "Any chance you can get more officers here?"

"They're on their way," Rameses said. "Of course, it would be easier if they would just close the terminal for a few hours so we can do our jobs, but God forbid we do anything to interrupt anyone's workday."

"How long before CSI gets here?" Faith asked.

"Fifteen minutes," Rameses said, "plus whatever time it takes for them to get past the crowd."

"We can't wait that long," Faith said. "People are going to figure out I'm just bluffing with Turk and then we're back to square one."

"Does it have to be a bluff?" Rameses asked. "I can look the other way if you feel inclined to send him after some of the lookie-loos."

Faith didn't bother to respond to that. "I'm going to take a look at the victim. You have gloves I can borrow?"

Rameses shook his head. "Only CSI and the coroner carry gloves."

"You don't have gloves in case you come across suspects with weapons or paraphernalia?"

"No," Rameses said. "Do you?"

"I have gloves," Michael said, pulling a pair of latex gloves from a pocket and sliding them on.

"Why are you carrying gloves?" Faith asked.

"In case we have to examine a body," Michael said. "Don't look surprised that I came prepared."

He knelt next to the body and said, "Okay, we have a male, early forties, Caucasian, looks to be about six-foot-two, 190 pounds, fairly good shape, although I'll know more when the coroner takes a look at him."

He carefully lifted the victim's head and checked for marks. From there, he proceeded to examine the rest of the body. It was covered by a thick, leather jacket above but nothing but shorts and high socks on his legs.

"I'm guessing the killer picked this outfit out as well," Michael said. "Not quite so fashionable an arrangement this time. More importantly, no sign of wounds or marks, although once more, we'll have to let the coroner take a look to be sure."

He rifled through the victim's pockets and said, "Well, pockets are empty. No ID. Did Chester have his wallet on him when he was found?"

"Sure did," Rameses said.

"So, either this is a different killer or he's learning," Michael said. "Although what he gains from lifting the man's wallet other than a couple hundred in cash is beyond me."

"A couple hundred in cash will carry you pretty far if you need it to," Rameses offered.

"And if this turns out to be unrelated to our first crime, I'll believe this was a mugging gone wrong. Until then, I'm going to go with the thought that the killer is trying to slow us down."

"How exactly will this slow us down?" Wales asked.

"Well," Michael said, standing, "when people are murdered, it's usually for a reason, and knowing who the victim is usually leads us to a reason."

"Oh," Wales said, reddening. "Right. Obviously."

"Don't beat yourself up," Rameses said sourly. "There's a reason he said *usually*."

"There's always a reason," Faith said. "It just doesn't always make sense. We can save the philosophy for another time though. We need to get this body out of here ASAP."

The crowd, realizing finally that Faith wasn't going to order Turk to attack a bunch of civilians, had begun to press closer to the scene again. The security team and police officers once more formed a barrier, but the crowd was far more zealous now than before, perhaps sensing that soon their body would be taken away from them, and they would miss their chance at immortalizing the moment they came across a real-life murder scene.

Lights flashed as cell phones captured the scene. Faith was fairly sure that her disgusted face and Michael's contemptuous one would end up on a lot of social media profiles before the day was out.

A few dozen yards away, just behind the crowd, a janitor watched the scene with the mildly irritated expression of a man who realized that his workday had just gotten a lot harder.

"Same, brother," Faith muttered under her breath.

Amy and her team showed up fifteen minutes later, along with two dozen more uniforms in riot gear. The riot officers were far rougher with the crowd than the rank-and-filers, but fortunately, the onlookers dissipated before they had to resort to non-lethal rounds.

Amy briefly conferred with the CSIs before telling her assistants to load the body onto the gurney for transportation. She walked over to the two agents, Rameses, and Wales and said, "Well, same as before, no marks, no signs of weaponry, nothing that might indicate any kind of harm at all. We'll do a full workup on him, but dollars to donuts the only thing we'll find is a needle mark and traces of phenol."

Faith glanced at the still-considerable crowd of onlookers and said, "Let's have the rest of this conversation at your office."

"Right," Amy said, scanning the crowd. "Guess there's nothing good on TV."

"What could possibly be as good as this?" Michael said sarcastically. "It's not every day you get to see a murder victim."

"If only that were true," Rameses said without a trace of humor.

An hour later, the five of them sat in a small meeting room at the coroner's office. The body lay in the next room. The full autopsy would take place later that day, but the preliminary examination proved them correct. The victim had been injected in the back of his neck, just above the hairline where Michael's cursory examination wouldn't reveal the wound. The toxicology report would have to wait for the full autopsy, but they were all certain that the report would come back positive for phenol.

"Do we have an ID yet?" Faith asked.

"We think so," Rameses said. "We didn't find a wallet or an ID of any kind, but the victim carried a pocketknife inscribed with E. Richardson. I did a search and the only E. Richardson who looks like our victim is one Everett Richardson, forty-two. The brother's on the way to confirm."

"So, our killer took his wallet but left his weapon?" Wales asked.

"Why disarm a man you've already killed?" Michael said. "He probably saw the knife and didn't think to check if it was inscribed."

"Maybe he was surprised," Faith said. "The terminal's open twenty-four hours now. We saw the other night that it's busy enough that it would be difficult to stage a body without being seen."

"I'll talk to my captain," Rameses said. "We can put out a bulletin and see if anyone noticed anything out of the ordinary. Maybe we'll get lucky, and someone will come forward with something useful."

"Do that," Faith said.

"Why would he stage the body in the same place?" Michael said. "Is he just toying with us?"

"Maybe," Faith said, "or maybe he works at the terminal. Or he just takes the same train as the victims, and he's connected to them somehow. We should wait until we interview the brother before we jump to any conclusions."

"I just don't get it," Michael said. "Killers normally hide their victims. Even when they stage them, like the Donkey Killer, they don't stage them in a crowded, public place. It's like this guy's begging to be caught."

"Or bragging that we can't catch him," Rameses posited.

"I could see that," Faith said. "He got away with it the first time, and now he needs the same rush, so he stages this victim near where the other one was killed so he can watch the crowd react."

"The crowd didn't react last time," Wales said. "There were a few people being crazy, but they were far fewer and more easily managed at the first scene. This, what I saw today, this was different. People were mobbing around like it was some kind of circus show."

"You'll get used to it," Rameses said.

Amy's cell phone buzzed. She answered, and after a moment, she nodded and said, "All right. Send him in."

She hung up and said, "Brother's here."

"All right," Rameses said. To the agents, he said, "Policy is that only the coroner and the next of kin can view the body. You two can wait in here, and Amy will send the brother in after the positive ID is confirmed. Wales and I will return to the station and see about getting that bulletin up. I wouldn't get your hopes up too much. Those things usually result in nothing but false leads."

"It only takes one good lead to make a difference," Faith encouraged them.

They left, and a moment later, Amy returned with a man who was clearly related to their victim, although a little younger and a little shorter. They watched through the window as Amy carefully pulled the sheet back from the victim. The brother sighed heavily and slumped forward, then nodded. Faith noted that he didn't seem surprised to see his brother dead. He did seem saddened, but mostly, he seemed frustrated and angry.

Amy talked with him a moment and pointed at the conference room door. He looked up and met Faith's eyes, and Faith saw defeat along with the other emotions mixed in. He had seen his brother's death coming. Faith was sure of it.

CHAPTER TWELVE

Amy led the brother into the room, and Faith noticed that Turk immediately walked to him and rubbed against his legs. The man smiled faintly and reached down to scratch behind his ears.

Faith couldn't officially rule him out as a suspect just yet, but Turk's instincts had been rock-solid so far. The uncomfortable memory of Turk leaping protectively in front of Faith as Ellie reached forward to embrace Faith flooded her mind. She pushed the image away and introduced them.

"I'm Special Agent Faith Bold," she said, "and this is Special Agent Michael Prince. That's our K9 unit, Turk."

"He's friendly," the man said. "Guess he doesn't suspect me." He looked up at the agents and said, "Sorry. I don't know why I said that. I guess I'm a little out of sorts."

"That's perfectly understandable," Faith said, "Mr. …"

"Oh, right," he said, "Sorry. I'm Blake Richardson. Everett's younger brother."

"Mr. Richardson, I'm sorry for your loss. Thank you for taking some time to speak with us."

"Yeah," he said, "of course."

They sat around the table, and Amy asked if anyone wanted coffee or water.

"I'll take coffee," Blake said. "Thank you."

Faith and Michael asked for water, and Amy disappeared to fetch the drinks. Faith asked, "Mr. Richardson, I'm so sorry to ask this, but can you verify your whereabouts yesterday evening?"

"Yeah," Blake said. "I was with my wife and daughter at home. They can verify that, but I don't know if it counts since they're my family. Maybe the neighbors saw me park and can confirm I didn't leave until this morning for work, but I don't know. People mind their own business. It's possible no one saw me. Sorry, I don't know why I'm talking so much."

"That's all right, Mr. Richardson," Faith said. "We'll follow up on that later."

Turk laid his head on Blake's lap, and Blake smiled faintly again. "Is he a therapy dog?"

"No," Faith said, "but he's pretty good at lifting people when they're down."

"Did he comfort you after you lost someone?" Blake asked.

"Not exactly," Faith said, "but he helped me overcome a very serious personal challenge. I can honestly say I wouldn't be where I am today without him."

Michael coughed, and Faith said, "But that's enough about me. Returning to your brother, Mr. Richardson, can you tell me if his behavior seemed different to you lately?"

"I wouldn't know," Blake said. "He and I weren't close."

Michael raised an eyebrow. "You two didn't get along?"

"We got along well enough when we saw each other," Blake said. "We just didn't see each other that often. My wife didn't care much for him, and I can't say I blame her."

"Why's that?" Faith asked.

Blake sighed. "My brother was challenging to be around. He wasn't a bad person, but he was very … well, he didn't care much who he offended."

"Can you explain?"

Blake sighed again. "Everett was … well, I guess the best way to put it is that he was indifferent to the effects his words had on others. He would say things sometimes that would offend people."

"Can you give us an example?"

"Well," Blake said, "There was a bad car accident a few years back. An SUV struck a woman and her baby. Killed the baby instantly and left the woman paralyzed from the neck down. Everett confessed to my wife and I that he visited the scene as soon as he heard the news to see if he could find the exact spot where the baby's head split open on the ground."

"Jesus," Michael said.

"Yeah," Blake said. "You see what I mean about him being hard to deal with."

"Did you have reason to suspect that your brother may have been involved in criminal activity?" Faith asked.

"You mean do I think he was a murderer because he was fascinated with death?"

"Was he?" Faith asked.

"Fascinated with death or a murderer?"

"Both."

"Well, I doubt like hell he ever murdered someone," Blake said. "He was all about what was convenient to him. He would fly into a rage if someone cut him off on the freeway and made him thirty seconds late to wherever he happened to be going. I could see him wanting to kill someone, but I can't see him bothering to go through the process of murdering someone. I don't know if I'm explaining myself well. I mean that he wasn't patient enough to be methodical, and he wouldn't put himself through the inconvenience of being convicted of murder and sentenced to prison."

"So, he wasn't a killer but that's only because he couldn't waste his own time?" Michael asked.

"Well, I don't know," Blake said. "I could be completely wrong, and he'd be just as horrified by murder as anyone. I just get the feeling that other people didn't matter much to him is all. I don't know. I'm a little out of sorts. I said that already, didn't I?"

Amy walked in with the drinks. She set the waters down in front of the agents and a cup of coffee in front of Blake, keeping one for herself. She stepped outside to allow the agents to finish their questioning.

Blake sipped his coffee and while he drank, Faith asked, "Can you think of anyone who might have wanted to hurt your brother?"

"Oh sure," he said. "Most of the people he met probably wanted to hurt him. There will be very few tears shed at his funeral, I'm afraid."

"Anyone who might have acted on that impulse?" Michael prodded.

"Hell, I don't know," he said. "I can tell you my wife and I wouldn't. We definitely wouldn't have killed him and dumped the body in one of the busiest subway terminals in the city."

Faith and Michael exchanged a glance. "How did you know where he was killed?"

"The coroner told me," he said. "Was she not supposed to?"

"No," Michael said, "but that's all right. Does the name Chester McIlhenny ring any bells?"

"No," Blake said. "Is that a friend of Everett's?"

"We were hoping you could tell us," Faith said.

"Sorry," Blake replied. "I don't know of a Chester McIlhenny."

"What about August Hornfeldt?"

"Hornfeldt? Isn't that the guy who would tase people to death?"

"That's him," Faith said. "Did you or your brother know him?"

"No," Blake said. "Why? Is this related somehow?"

"We're just trying to see if there's any connection between your brother's death and another case we're working on," Faith said.

"What case?" Realization dawned on him, and he said, "Wait, is Chester McIlhenny that old guy they found dead in the subway a few days ago? Did the same killer kill my brother?"

"Let's not jump to any conclusions," Faith said. "We're still in the beginning stages of the investigation."

"Why?" Blake said. "I mean, if it is the same killer, then why? It doesn't make sense. I mean, unless that guy knew McIlhenny from somewhere else and is just offing people he doesn't like."

"It's possible," Faith said. "Did your brother take an interest in the case at all? Hornfeldt's case, I mean."

"Not that I know of," Blake said, "but like I said, Everett and I weren't close."

Faith nodded. "Thank you for your time, Mr. Richardson. If you think of anything else, please give us a call. Again, please accept my condolences for your loss."

She handed Blake a card, and he left the room. He paused in front of his brother's body—covered once more with the sheet—then allowed Amy to lead him from the autopsy studio.

"Well," Michael said, "what do you think?"

"I don't think this is related to the Hornfeldt case at all," Faith said. "Richardson wasn't even remotely involved with the case. It's possible they had a mutual acquaintance, but failing that, the only thing we know for sure that connects them is that they were both found in the same area of the Twin Cities Terminal."

"So, an employee or a regular passenger who uses that platform," Michael said.

"Possibly."

Michael sighed. "So, there could possibly only be several hundred thousand suspects."

"That's better than twenty million," Faith offered.

Michael didn't find that observation funny.

***

"How is it possible that not a single security camera faces this entire platform?" Michael asked.

"Well, we cover the coffee cart, ticketing counter, and boarding area," Sita said. "We feel that's adequate coverage."

"Do you still feel that way?" Michael asked.

Sita didn't respond to that.

Faith and Michael had returned to the terminal after wrapping up at the coroner's office. With no connection between their victims but the terminal, they decided their time was best spent looking for leads there. Their first stop upon arriving was visiting the security office. Sita had promised Michael she would look into footage of the night McIlhenny was killed but hadn't yet gotten back to him.

Now, Faith knew why. The security cameras at the terminal were woefully inadequate. They covered high traffic areas well enough, but there were plenty of places with no coverage at all, including the majority of the platform where McIlhenny and Richardson were found.

"That's an employee only area," Sita explained. "We didn't think we'd need to monitor that area."

"So, your employees are immune to criminal activity?" Michael challenged, irritated.

"We vet our employees very well," Sita said. "Full background checks for everyone."

"If I had all day, I could list the number of people who've had full background checks and turned out to be murderers," Michael said, "for God's sake, Miss Bhandari."

"What do you want me to say?" she said, lifting her hands in frustration. "We don't sit at board meetings thinking 'How can we aim our security cameras to catch any potential murderers who might be planting bodies in our busiest platform?'"

"How's that working out for you?" Michael asked irritably.

"Drop it, Michael," Faith finally said. "They don't have footage. Arguing about it won't change that."

Michael glared at Faith. Sita cast a smug glance at him.

Her smug look vanished when Faith met her eyes. "Miss Bhandari, you should know that at this point in time, we believe that the murderer is an employee of yours."

"An employee? Here? That's not possible!"

"I'm afraid it is," Faith said. "Granted, the security system you have is inadequate, but it's still incredibly unlikely that the killer could have managed to kill and stage two individuals without being noticed by other staff, passengers, or any of the security cameras in the terminal at all. The only explanation that makes any kind of sense is that the killer is familiar with the security setup here and knew how to avoid detection. That means an employee."

"Well, what about the people who constructed the terminal?" Sita said. "Couldn't one of them be the killer?"

"Miss Bhandari, this terminal was constructed in 1914," Faith said, "and the last remodel took place in 1929. There have been touchups since then, but this particular platform hasn't had any new infrastructure installed in thirty years."

Sita sighed and ran her hands through her hair. "This is impossible," she said.

"And yet," Michael quipped.

Sita was silent a moment. Then she said, "What would you like to do?"

Faith was about to say that she wanted to interview her employees, starting with those assigned to this platform, but before she could, Turk began to bark loudly.

Faith turned to see Turk staring down a tall, burly man walking across the platform. When he saw the dog, his eyes widened in alarm.

Faith frowned and called, "Sir! FBI. I need to talk to you."

The man looked up and met Faith's eyes for a brief moment. Then he sprinted away.

Turk looked at Faith, and Faith nodded. "Get him, boy! Stop him!"

Turk chased the man, passing a surprised-looking janitor pushing a cart of cleaning supplies. Faith followed him, recalling the last time Turk reacted to a random stranger. That stranger turned out to be a serial killer who nearly killed another victim because Faith prevented Turk from stopping him when he recognized his scent in a public park.

She wouldn't make that mistake again.

CHAPTER THIRTEEN

Faith knew a thing or two about strength under duress. She had experienced it many times herself in the Marine Corps and the FBI. So, it wasn't particularly surprising that the man Turk chased somehow gained almost superhuman speed and agility despite being a solid twenty pounds overweight and at least ten years older than Faith herself.

But God, it was annoying. Three times Turk closed enough to leap at the man and three times, the man pivoted like a dancer, avoiding Turk's snapping jaws and gaining distance from his pursuers.

"Stop!" Faith cried, drawing her weapon. "FBI!"

She didn't chamber a round yet. She couldn't fire the weapon in a crowded train terminal like this. Even if she were a crack shot, the risk of hitting an innocent person was too high.

She could only hope that the suspect didn't know that.

Either he did know that, or he didn't, but he was willing to risk his life because he looked back at Faith and saw the gun but didn't so much as slow down. He leapt over a short retaining wall into a narrow maintenance corridor that ran alongside the tracks.

Her bluff called, Faith holstered her weapon and sprinted after the guy. Turk leapt easily down the corridor, and Faith followed. Above her, she heard Michael call, "I'm going to head to the next platform and try to cut him off! Watch out for trains!"

"Gee, thanks for the advice," Faith muttered.

Turk leapt once more at the guy, and this time, he managed to sink his teeth into the man's arm. "Yes!" Faith cried. "Bring him down, boy!"

The man screamed in pain and terror and, with yet another display of superhuman strength, flung Turk off of him.

Instead of continuing to run, he stopped, and after glancing at Faith to make sure she was too far away to reach him, he planted a solid kick into Turk's ribs. Turk yelped and tumbled onto the tracks.

"No!" Faith cried. "Turk, be careful!"

The subway was powered by a high-voltage central rail in between the two track rails. If Turk touched that rail, he would be instantly shocked to death.

Faith grabbed the handrail of the maintenance corridor and prepared to vault over the side to rescue her dog, but Turk's intuition once more proved flawless. He leapt over the central rail and then bounded up onto the maintenance walkway and charged after the man.

"Good boy!" Faith called. "Get that bastard!"

She was angry now. It was one thing to run from Turk, but to try to kill him? That was a mistake Faith would make sure he paid for.

The suspect had done an incredible job so far of outrunning his pursuers, but his luck was running out. Underneath the tunnel with nothing but the deadly electricity of the tracks to his left, there was nowhere for him to go but straight ahead, and his initial burst of adrenaline faded fast, leaving him huffing and slowing rapidly. Still, he managed to fend off another leap from Turk, kicking backwards and catching the dog midleap. The blow only glanced Turk and didn't do any damage, but it was enough to throw him off balance, so he landed heavily on the ground and tumbled end over end.

Faith drew her weapon, once more not intending to use it but hoping that in this confined space and in his state of exhaustion, he would decide that surrender was more prudent than fighting.

"Stop!" she cried. "FBI!"

The suspect didn't stop, but Faith holstered her weapon anyway. He had finally run out of gas. He reached the open air of the next platform and tried weakly to climb the rail to the passenger waiting area but couldn't lift himself up. Turk leapt onto him, grabbing his arm and wrestling him to the ground.

"Help!" he cried out, his voice breathy and almost squeaky. "Help me! Please!"

Faith jogged toward them, and when she saw Michael skid to a stop in front of them and train his handgun on the suspect, she called Turk off of him.

"Help!" the man called again. Faith could detect a faint trace of accent, though it was hard to tell how much of that was terror and how much was an actual difference in language.

"Stay still!" Faith said, pulling her cuffs from her pocket.

The man looked at her with frightened eyes and said—and this time the accent was unmistakable—"Why are you arresting me? What did I do?"

“You’re not under arrest,” Faith said. “You’re being detained for questioning regarding the murders of Chester McIlhenny and Everett Richardson. Roll over onto your stomach.”

“Who? I don’t know these men!”

“You can tell me all about it in a few minutes. Give me your left hand.”

“Faith?” Michael called. “We have a problem.”

Faith looked up and saw the crowd gathering around them. This crowd was rapidly growing to the same size as the one around Richardson’s body earlier today, and within minutes, they would be just as rambunctious.

“Stand up,” Faith said, puling the suspect to his feet. “Michael, call Miss Bhandari. Tell her we have a suspect on the maintenance walkway in front of Platform …” she looked up, “… 12B. Tell her we’re moving him, and we need someone to open the maintenance room for us to talk to him. If we can get security presence that would be nice too.”

“Will do,” Michael said.

“All right, sir,” Faith said to her suspect. “Walk with me.”

She walked the suspect away from the crowd toward the next tunnel. Turk followed close behind, glancing every few seconds into the crowd to ensure that the crowd wasn’t threatening them.

They reached the maintenance entrance under the next tunnel, and Faith called Michael. “ETA?”

“Any second now,” Michael said. “We’re in the maintenance corridor as we speak.”

“Good.”

“What did I do?” the suspect whined. “I don’t know these men.”

“We’ll talk in a moment,” Faith said.

“Can you take the cuffs off?”

“No.”

“This isn’t right!” he whined. “I have rights! I study America! I know you can’t hold me without a warrant!”

The maintenance door opened, and Faith led the suspect into a room where Michael and two massive security guards waited. The room was little more than a supply closet and with everyone inside, they were crowded to the point where they couldn’t move.

“Is there anywhere else to go?” Faith asked.

“There’s a break room close by,” one of the officers said. “We’ll take you there.”

The suspect continued to whine about his cuffs as they walked to the break room. Michael dropped back until he was next to Faith. "You two all right?"

"We're fine," Faith said. "He threw Turk onto the tracks, but thankfully for our suspect here, Turk missed the electrified rail."

"I didn't mean to electrocute him," the man whined. "He bit my arm!"

They reached the break room, and Faith told the security guards to wait outside and secure the room until they were finished. Once that was done, the suspect said quietly, "Can you please take my cuffs off? I won't run, I promise."

"I believe you," Faith said, "but since you resisted detainment and behaved violently with my K9 unit, I can't take the cuffs off until we're finished. It's Bureau policy."

"He attacked me!" the man protested.

"He attacked you after you started running," Faith said.

"I started running because a vicious dog was growling at me! What would you have done?"

"I would have asked the nice woman in the bulletproof vest marked FBI to restrain her dog," Faith said. "I wouldn't have run and then ignored her every command to stop."

"What do you expect me to do?" the suspect protested. "I've done nothing wrong, and you sic your dog on me?"

"If you've done nothing wrong," Faith said, "then you have my sincerest apologies."

She helped the man sit on one of the chairs then took the one opposite him. Michael remained standing while Turk sat by the door and watched the suspect quietly.

"All right," Faith said. "Do you consent to recording this conversation?"

The suspect nodded. "All right."

"Thank you," Faith said.

She set her cell phone on the table and started recording. "Please state your name for the record."

"Adiel Schoenmaker."

"Mr. Schoenmaker, where are you from?"

"Johannesburg, South Africa."

"And how long have you been in the United States?"

"Three days. I am here for a business convention."

Three days. That was marginal. Chester McIlhenny was killed early in the morning, technically closer to four days ago than three days ago.

"Exactly what time did you arrive?" Michael said.

"I landed at 11:29 a.m.," he said. "LaGuardia Airport. Flight … uh … I believe it was United Airlines Flight 2595."

Michael pulled his phone from his pocket and looked up the flight. While he did, Faith asked, "What do you do for work, Mr. Schoenmaker?"

"I am a chemist," he said. "I work for Internasionale Chemiese Oplossings. I'm here for a convention."

"What sort of chemicals do you make?"

"Medical supplies," he said.

"Like phenol?"

"Yes, like phenol and many other chemicals." His brow furrowed. "We're known primarily for phenol and associated compounds though. How did you know this? Are you familiar with our organization?"

"Mr. McIlhenny and Mr. Richardson were killed with an injection of pure phenol," Faith said. "You're not aware of this?"

Schoenmaker's eyes widened. "Pure phenol? That would be nearly instantaneous!"

"It was," Faith said. "Can you account for your whereabouts during your stay in the United States?"

"I was at the convention," he said. "It was held at the Grand River Hotel Resort on Staten Island. I was there all day, and at night, I was at the hotel. I went sightseeing today, and I head home tomorrow." His eyes widened. "Will I be held here? Will I miss my flight?"

Michael sighed before Faith could answer. "Do you have any form of ID on you, Mr. Schoenmaker?"

"Yes, my passport. It's in my rear pocket."

Michael helped him stand and retrieved the passport. He glanced at it, then nodded, and put the document back in Schoenmaker's pocket. "All right, Mr. Schoenmaker. I've confirmed you were on a flight at the time of Mr. McIlhenny's death, so you are cleared as a suspect. I apologize for the confusion."

Faith sighed and pursed her lips but quickly regained control of her professionalism. "I apologize for my mistake, Mr. Schoenmaker. Would you like us to obtain medical care for you?"

"No, please, I just want to go back to my hotel."

"All right," Faith said. "We'll have you escorted to a different platform and placed on a train to your hotel. Thank you for your cooperation."

"I didn't really have a choice, did I?" he said with just the slightest hint of irritation.

Faith didn't answer him.

***

"So, Turk screwed up?" Michael asked.

Faith took a deep breath and said, "Yeah, looks like it."

Michael nodded. "Well, he probably smelled the phenol and thought it was the killer."

"Yeah," Faith said, "that's my guess."

"Don't feel bad about it. Everyone makes mistakes. You, too, Turk," he said, ruffling his head. "Don't feel bad."

Faith sighed. She knew a part of Michael was happy that Turk had misidentified the killer because it meant he could be wrong about Ellie too. She didn't begrudge him this, but it wasn't guilt over Ellie that soured her mood.

"I don't feel bad, Michael," she said. "I feel frustrated."

"Yeah, I get that."

They were enjoying a late lunch at the food court on the ground floor of the terminal. Or rather, they were eating a late lunch. Though the stir-fried beef and vegetables and lo mein noodles were actually a step up from most of the fast-food Chinese Faith had tried, Faith wasn't in much of an enjoying mood.

"So, where do we go from here?" Michael asked after a moment.

"We need to establish a motive," Faith said. "It's possible that this is just location-based, and we're dealing with a psycho who gets off on planting dead people on benches, but I think it's more involved than that."

"So, why these victims?" Michael asked rhetorically.

"Exactly," she said. "Everett Richardson was a jerk, so it makes sense that people would want him dead, but we don't know if Chester McIlhenny was the same."

"We know he was estranged from his family," Faith said. "Maybe there's a reason for that."

"Have you talked to his kids yet?" Michael asked.

"No," Faith admitted. "I was distracted by the discovery of Richardson's body."

"Well, let's talk to them," Michael said. "You still have the contact info?"

Faith checked her phone. "Yeah, I got it right here."

"Anyone local?"

"The oldest son, Brandon. He has a New York phone number. Not sure if he's still here, but I'll try him first."

Brandon was, in fact, local. He worked as a foreman in a plastics factory in Greenpoint. He agreed to meet the agents near his office.

The agents were quiet on the drive over. Faith realized that she missed talking with Michael. They used to joke and banter with each other like friends, but lately, these periods of silence were the most comfortable they felt with each other. Faith wondered if part of her dislike of Ellie could be due to the fact that she was jealous of her for pulling Michael away. She didn't feel jealous, but she knew that sometimes jealousy could manifest in different ways. Maybe she was finding reasons to be wary of Ellie because she missed Michael's friendship and blamed Ellie for the growing rift between them.

She would ask Doctor West about it when they returned home. For now, she would focus on the case.

They reached the factory in fifteen minutes, a minor miracle in New York traffic. Brandon McIlhenny met them in the lobby and led them to the building's cafeteria.

He ordered a coffee for himself and one for each of the agents. "The dog drink coffee?" he asked with a slight smile.

When the agents didn't return his smile, he shrugged and said, "Just a joke. I used to have a German shepherd when I was a kid. Best dog breed on the planet."

"I agree," Faith said with a smile.

They sat at a table a little removed from the other diners so they could talk in relative privacy.

"So," Brandon said, "you're here to talk about my father."

"Yes," Faith said. "We apologize for taking so long to get to you."

"I understand," Brandon said. "You had that other body to deal with."

"Yes," Faith said. "How did you know about that?"

"It's all over the news," Brandon said. "They're calling him the Subway Vampire. People are claiming he drains the blood from his victims and leaves their exsanguinated corpses for passengers to find."

Michael rolled his eyes. Faith chuckled softly and said, "Well, the truth is only slightly less dramatic, but you know all about that."

"Yes," Brandon said, his hands tightening around his mug. "Yes, I do."

"Mr. McIlhenny—"

"Please," Brandon said, "that was my father. I'm just Brandon. Or Brandy."

"Brandon," Faith said, "I hate to ask you this, but can you think of a reason why someone might want to hurt your father?"

Brandon sighed. He sipped his coffee and tapped the table with his finger. "My first instinct is to say no, but … well, I suppose if he pissed off the wrong person, then yes, someone might want to hurt him."

"Did your father often get into arguments with people?" Faith asked.

Brandon chuckled. "Well, yeah, I suppose you could say that," he said, "at least when I knew him. He had a real mean streak. A *real* mean streak. That's why we don't talk to him anymore. Didn't talk to him."

"You and your brother and sister?"

"Yes," Brandon said. "He used to belittle us almost constantly. Mostly over our career choices, but he used to be very hard on Elizabeth. She married a man who owns a gas station franchise. According to my father, that was beneath her."

"I see," Faith said. "I'm sorry to hear that."

"So was my sister," Brandon said.

"Did you have any contact with your father at all after your mother's death?"

He shrugged. "Well, you know, text messages on birthdays and Christmas. A phone call here and there. Not much. Nothing since last year. He was on the jury for the Hornfeldt case, so he didn't talk to us. He took his civic duty very seriously."

"So, you don't know of anyone specifically who might have disliked him?"

"No," Brandon said. "And to be fair, I don't even know if anyone disliked him anymore. For all I know, he was perfectly pleasant to anyone who wasn't his family. Have you tried his coworkers?"

"We'll try them next," Faith said. "Thank you."

They tried his coworkers and got the same information. Had a mean streak, very judgmental. No, no one in particular wanted to kill him. No one missed him all that much, but they didn't hate him enough to do anything about it.

They reached the hotel just in time for a dinner as joyless as their lunch. To occupy himself, Michael verified alibis for the people who worked in Chester's department. As expected, they were all solid.

"Wonderful," Faith said. "Back to square one."

"Not exactly," Michael said. "We know that both of our victims were jerks. If our killer is opportunistic and he does work at the terminal, then he could be targeting people who are rude to him."

"Possibly," Faith said.

"It's worth a shot, at least, Faith."

"Yeah," she agreed. "God, I'm getting sick of saying that."

"Yeah, me too."

They lapsed once more into silence. Faith picked at her food and thought of the nickname the press had given their killer.

The Subway Vampire. Like he was some kind of movie character. It was disgusting. It took people hours to realize McIlhenny was dead, and now, they were glorifying his killer. Maybe he was a jerk, but he didn't deserve to be nothing more than a footnote in an article celebrating a psychopath.

"I'll follow up with some of his other coworkers," Michael said. "Maybe one of them has an idea who might have a grievance to McIlhenny bad enough to want him dead."

"You do that," Faith said, standing from the table. "I'm going to shower."

In her younger days, she would have been able to convince herself to be optimistic about Michael's chances of finding something, but it had been a long time since she felt optimistic about anything.

CHAPTER FOURTEEN

He figured it out now. He knew his mistake. He had pushed the bounds of indifference too far. He'd forgotten that people enjoyed spectacle, that spectacle was the only thing that could crack the veneer of indifference that society had.

He shouldn't have dressed his victims up as caricatures. He had gotten lucky with the first one. People were on the lookout for weirdly dressed individuals who weren't moving now. They wanted to see their spectacle.

He would be more careful next time. He would keep the victim in the clothes they wore, adding only a pair of sunglasses or a hat to keep their eyes hidden. After all, people were inclined to notice something out of the ordinary. It was the ordinary they ignored, the normal people who they didn't care about.

Like this man in front of him. He brushed past a young lady without so much as a glance her way, not even when she cried out in frustration as her purse went sailing through the air at the impact.

The young lady wasn't particularly attractive. Her clothes weren't particularly expensive. She wore no jewelry. There was nothing about her that would attract anyone's attention. Nothing except the fact that she was human, a living, breathing creature with rights and dignity who should be granted the respect due everyone.

Of course, without at least the vague promise of sex or money or prestige, no one received respect. That was the problem.

He followed the man, pushing his cart and looking around, seemingly absently. Really, he was trying to see if he would be noticed. The terminal was crowded, but people weren't looking his way. Janitors in public places were part of the furniture. He could probably shout, "Hey guys! I'm going to kill someone!" and no one would glance his way.

Still, he had made his mistake already. It would be foolish of him to make another one.

He would have to act fast. There was a bench up ahead, not too far from them. He had the phenol in his cart. He kept it there while he worked since each janitor had their own cart, and he could hide it among all the cleaning chemicals. He could catch up to him, jab him quickly in the neck, and help him sit before anyone saw him. If anyone did see him, he would simply be apologizing for accidentally bumping into a passenger. It would be challenging to plant sunglasses on him, but that could be done without if needed. He could position him with his head slumped forward as though he were taking a nap.

He increased his pace just slightly. Just enough to catch up to his victim right as they reached the bench. One quick jab, then he could slowly lower him to the bench.

He reached into his cart for the needle, his heartbeat quickening.

"Help!" a voice cried.

He froze and turned toward the sound to see a large man running from a big dog, a German shepherd. The dog wore a vest with a gold K9 emblazoned on it. Both were quickly followed by an attractive, physically fit woman in her early thirties wearing a bulletproof vest emblazoned with FBI on the back.

He recognized her from yesterday, one of the FBI agents who was investigating the murders. She glanced his way as she ran past but didn't show any sign of suspicion or even acknowledgement.

Well, why would she acknowledge him? He was just a janitor after all. Just another piece of the furniture.

He looked back at his would-be victim. He stood right in front of the bench. With everyone's attention focused on the FBI agent and her dog, he could easily kill the man and stage him before anyone even looked his way.

He wouldn't, though. There was no point. If no one noticed his victim because there was a spectacle distracting them, then that wouldn't prove anything. The point was to show everyone how little attention they paid to others, not to just get away with killing. He would wait until the right time, a time when people should notice a dead body but wouldn't because, unless it directly involved them, it wasn't worth their time.

He was a teacher, after all, not a psychopath.

He watched with the crowd until the man and the woman and dog chasing him disappeared from view. Then he resumed pushing his cart. He passed his would-be victim on the bench and smiled at him, nodding politely.

The man didn't even notice he was there.

"Just another piece of furniture," he muttered to himself as he faced forward and continued to push his cart.

CHAPTER FIFTEEN

"It has to be someone who works here," Faith said. "The only connection between the victims is that they're both jerks and they both used the terminal."

"Well," Michael said, "that narrows our suspect pool from hundreds of thousands to hundreds. That's progress."

"Sure," Faith said, "I suppose it is."

They sat in the security office at the terminal reviewing footage from the night of Chester McIlhenny's death. They were grasping at straws considering the woeful camera coverage, but if they could catch sight of either of the victims, they could at least get a sense of the timeline and hopefully an idea of where the actual murders took place.

"Can you call the field office?" Faith said. "Have them start looking into the employees here. See if anyone has a violent criminal past."

"Sure," Michael said.

Just at that moment, his phone buzzed. He picked it up and frowned. "Shit."

"What is it?"

"The Boss," Michael said. He answered and said, "Prince. Yeah, she's here."

He set the phone down on the desk and put it on speaker.

"Hi, Boss," Faith said, steeling herself for what she knew would be an unpleasant conversation.

She was right.

"What the hell are you two doing over there? I just got a call from the South African consulate saying you brutalized a South African citizen? You sicced your K9 on him and detained him without cause?"

"That's not true, sir," Faith said. "Turk smelled the poison on him and chased him down only after he refused to stop. We interrogated him briefly, and once we determined he wasn't involved, we offered medical care, which Mr. Schoenmaker declined, and then we released him."

"So, he did maul Mr. Schoenmaker. Why the hell was he detained in the first place?"

"Because, sir," Faith said, "he refused to stop."

"And why did he run, Bold?" the Boss asked irritably. "Did you politely approach him and ask to question him? Or perhaps Turk lunged at him the moment he caught a scent, and you demanded that he stop on that pretense. Then, when Schoenmaker ran from the aggressive woman and her snarling German shepherd, you just let Turk run Mr. Schoenmaker down because hey, he smelled something so it must be our killer."

Faith sighed and said, "Yes, sir."

"Yes, what?"

Faith sighed again. "Yes, Turk chased him, and I … allowed the pursuit."

"Lovely," the Boss said. "Well, you're suspended."

"What?" Michael and Faith said together.

"Yeah, you're suspended. Or you would be if Mr. Schoenmaker decided to press charges. You allowed your K9 unit to fly completely off the handle and injure a citizen of another nation on a cause that is as thin as anything I've ever heard. Mr. Schoenmaker is well within his rights to sue the FBI for mistreatment, which would have cost us potentially hundreds of thousands of dollars in legal fees, damages, and medical care."

"So, I'm not suspended?" Faith asked.

"I'm so glad you're understanding the salient points of this conversation, Bold," the Boss said sarcastically. "No, you're not suspended, but full disclosure, Bold, I was typing up your suspension when Clark convinced me not to."

"Clark convinced you not to suspend me?"

"Yes," the Boss said. "He pointed out that if your little escapade had worked, then there would be no reason to suspend you. Can't say I agree with that logic, but he also pointed out that you and Prince have the best track record for solving these spree killings and moving the case over to the New York office would delay resolution of this case. Unfortunately, I do agree with that, so you get to keep your job, but Bold, you are on ice so thin if you so much as sneeze, it'll collapse underneath you. For the last time, get your shit together."

"Yes, sir," Faith said quietly.

"And get a handle on your K9. He should know better than to just rush after someone without a command to pursue."

Faith's jaw tightened slightly. "Yes, sir."

"Sir, before you go," Michael said, "can you get records to look up some backgrounds for me."

"As usual, you're a pain in my ass, Prince," the Boss said, "but thankfully for you, you're doing actual investigative work and not running people down with your big bad wolf, so yes, I'll talk to records. What's the name?"

"Well, sir, it's everyone who works for the Twin Cities Terminal."

After a moment of silence, the Boss sighed. "Glad to see you've narrowed the list down so much," he said sarcastically.

"Also," Michael said, "it was actually Faith's idea to check on the people who work here."

"Your loyalty is admirable, Prince," the Boss said, "but I truly don't give a shit. She's on notice, and so are you if you're not careful. Start thinking about your future, Prince."

He hung up, and the two agents sat in silence for a while. Faith replayed the Boss's last sentence over in her head. *Start thinking about your future, Prince.* The implied message was that perhaps his future would be more secure without Bold.

After a moment, Faith stood and said, "I'm going to get some air. Call me if you find something."

"Hey, Faith, he doesn't really mean that. About being careful around you."

"Yes, he does," Faith said.

Turk started to follow, but she said, "Stay here."

Turk sat slowly, confused. Faith felt a pang of guilt. None of this was Turk's fault, but she needed a moment to herself.

She could understand the Boss's frustration. The fact that Schoenmaker wasn't a U.S. Citizen made the situation incredibly embarrassing. The Boss hadn't mentioned a media circus, and Faith knew that meant Schoenmaker had requested to avoid a media circus.

She couldn't even be angry with Schoenmaker for talking to his consulate. That was standard legal advice when accused of a crime in a foreign country, even when cleared almost immediately. It was good advice too. He had acted correctly.

Turk hadn't. That was the part that frustrated Faith. Turk should have waited for her command to chase the suspect. He should have alerted her, but he shouldn't have chased him without Faith's permission.

Well, the last time Faith had prevented him from chasing a suspect, that suspect had nearly murdered another victim, so Faith couldn't really be mad at herself for allowing Turk to follow his instincts. What was worse, detaining someone briefly or allowing a killer to kill again.

That way lies danger, she thought to herself. She could allow herself to be angry. She could allow herself to be frustrated and even to feel humiliated, but she couldn't start justifying procedural mistakes. She would have to refresh Turk's training a little to avoid instances like this.

And she would have to stop being a cowboy. She recalled her conversation with Doctor West prior to her assignment to this case. He suggested that Faith possibly sought physical confrontation to make up for her lack of control when Trammell tortured her. She didn't feel that way when she chased Schoenmaker, but maybe that was another subconscious act.

"God, this sucks," she said out loud.

A middle-aged woman waiting for her train glanced Faith's way. Faith smiled and lifted her hand, then turned around and headed back for the security office. Her little break hadn't improved her mood, and she saw no point in continuing to isolate herself.

When she returned, Turk jumped to his feet and rushed to her, whining plaintively. "Hey, buddy," she said, stooping and scratching him under his chin. "I'm sorry. Mommy's just a little upset. It's not your fault."

Turk licked her hands and pressed close for a hug. Faith held him a long moment, and when she released him, she felt a little better. Not much, but enough to put her irritation aside and focus on the case.

"Anything on the background checks yet?" she asked Michael.

"Nothing so far," he replied. "A lot of the maintenance and janitorial staff have minor records but nothing more recent than five years and nothing more major than petty theft."

"Yeah, I figured," Faith said. "What about the cameras?"

"Nope. Nothing."

Faith sighed. "Yeah, I figured that too."

She looked at the screen and frowned. "Hold on. Pause the video right there."

Michael pressed a button, and the video froze. "What is it?"

"Right there," Faith said, pointing at an older man walking into the bathroom nearest the spot where the bodies were found. "Is that McIlhenny?"

Michael peered closely. "Well, what do you know," he said.

He rewound the footage fifteen seconds, and they both watched as Chester entered the bathroom. Three minutes later, he exited.

"Okay," Michael said. "Timestamp is 5:33. We know that he was staged on the bench by the time Kylie Bonaparte arrived for work at 5:45. That gives us a twelve-minute window after he leaves the bathroom until he's killed and staged. That means the poisoning either happened in the bathroom or right after he left the bathroom."

"Let's check the day Richardson was killed," Faith said. "We can see if he uses the same restroom."

Twenty minutes later, they confirmed that not only did Richardson use the same restroom, but he used it approximately ten minutes before his own body was found.

"It would have to be almost immediately after using the restroom," Faith said. "The killer changed both of them into different outfits."

"Where, though?" Michael asked. "He didn't take them back into the bathroom."

"Best guess is a maintenance room or supply closet," Faith said. "Although that leaves the question again of how he managed to do it without being noticed."

"Let me go back a little bit," Michael said. "Maybe we missed something."

They reviewed the footage again, slowing it down and checking each frame from the time each victim entered the restroom to the time they left. Chester's video revealed nothing, but when they viewed Richardson's footage again, Faith caught a glimpse of something in the frame just as Richardson left the restroom.

"Stop!" she cried. "There."

She pointed just inside the bathroom door where a hand could be seen extended, a towel hanging from the arm to which the hand attached. "What's that?" Michael asked. "A restroom attendant?"

"Looks like it," Faith said.

"Here? Why?"

Faith shrugged. "It gives people the impression of luxury."

Michael shook his head, "I guess. I don't know, I feel like I'd rather handle drying my own hands after using the toilet."

"I'm with you there," Faith said. She stopped and thought a moment. "In fact," she said, "I imagine most people using this terminal would feel the same way. I further imagine that most people would ignore our poor restroom attendant, maybe even brush past them rudely in their haste to avoid an interaction they would find uncomfortable."

Realization dawned on Michael, "And our two victims were rather known for rudeness. Perhaps our neglected restroom attendant couldn't handle this latest insult to the injury of a job that involves helping people after they void their bowels and decided to take his frustration out on them in a violent way."

"Call Miss Bhandari," Faith said. "I want to know who this restroom attendant is. I want to talk to him."

CHAPTER SIXTEEN

"I have a very hard time believing that anyone in my employ could be responsible for these violent acts."

Michael took a breath to calm himself before he said, "Miss Bhandari, I appreciate the difficult position you're in, but we can't refrain from investigating a lead because you have a hard time accepting it. I need the restroom attendant's contact information."

"Please, Special Agent, I would feel more comfortable if we went through the police. There are procedures to follow, policies—"

"That procedure, Miss Bhandari, is getting a warrant and subpoenaing your employment records. Now we can do that if you insist, but if we do, two things will happen: one, your name will be on a lot of documents stating that you refused to cooperate with a federal investigation. Two, we will find and question your employee anyway, with or without your permission. You're not helping anyone by playing difficult, least of all yourself."

The first statement was bending the truth a little, but Michael had no more patience for Sita Bhandari. He understood her desire to avoid bad publicity, and he understood that her superiors would likely take out any frustration on her, but people were dying, and he really couldn't care less about propriety or politics right now.

Sita sighed heavily and said, "All right. The attendant's name is Leon Presley. He's on duty at the moment in the same restroom. I'll send him to you."

"That's all right," Michael said. "We'll go to him. Thank you, Miss Bhandari."

"Of course."

Michael hung up, and the three of them left the security office and headed for the restroom. The terminal was still busy with the last of the evening rush, and there was a line to enter. Michael flashed his badge, but that only succeeded in irritating the people in line.

Turk growled softly, and the line finally gave way. Michael passed the muttering people in line and headed into the restroom. He found Presley standing next to the towel dispenser, an empty tip jar to his left, and a resigned expression on his face.

"Leon Presley?" Michael asked.

Presley turned lazily to Michael. When he saw the FBI logo on Michael's jacket and the K9 vest on Turk, he froze. His face paled, and he said, "Oh shit!" then sprinted out of the restroom.

He knocked Michael on his way out, shoving him against the wall. Turk snapped at him and started to lunge, but then stopped and looked at Faith.

"Go get him," Faith said. "Take him down."

Turk sprinted after Presley, with Michael and Faith hot on his heels.

"Stop!" Michael called. "FBI!"

Presley looked behind him then picked up the pace. "Dammit," Michael muttered, increasing the speed of his pursuit.

Schoenmaker was an overweight man approaching middle age. Presley was younger than Michael's thirty-eight years of age and in much better shape than Schoenmaker. It became clear almost immediately that Michael wouldn't catch him. Faith, a daily jogger, outpaced Michael, but she also couldn't match Presley's raw speed.

Turk, of course, had no problem reaching Presley, catching him just before he reached an employee entrance.

But not soon enough. Presley rushed through the door and pushed it shut just as Turk leaped. Turk crashed into the door and fell to the ground with a yelp. He quickly rolled over and regained his feet, but Presley was gone.

Michael opened the door and caught him rounding a corner at the end of a long hallway. He rushed after him, drawing his weapon and calling, "Stop! FBI!"

Behind Michael, he could hear Faith and Turk following him. "Call security!" Michael said. "Tell them to stop Presley if they see him!"

Michael chased Presley into a crowded break room. The other employees looked up in surprise at the commotion. Presley slowed to a walk and tried to hide himself in the crowd, but Michael picked him out easily and approached swiftly. After a moment, Presley looked up and swore, then sprinted toward the room door, shoving past people, knocking several to the ground.

"Stop!" Michael called, "FBI!"

The crowded employees somehow managed to get into Michael's way at every turn, and by the time he left the break room, Presley was well ahead of him, heading for the parking garage.

"Shit!" Michael called. "He's going for his car!"

He sprinted after Presley with every ounce of his strength, but he knew it wouldn't be enough. "Turk! Get him!" he called.

Turk rushed past Michael, ears flat and tail pointed straight behind him as he pursued Presley.

Presley turned and prepared to kick Turk, but Michael lifted his weapon and said, "You kick that dog, I'll put one in your knee!"

Faith glanced at Michael in alarm, but Michael ignored her. "Stay where you are!" Michael said. "Stay there!"

Presley looked at Michael, eyes white with fear. Turk reached him, and Faith called, "Hold!"

Turk stopped just before leaping at Presley and stood his ground, growling menacingly at him.

"Okay!" Presley called, eyes white with fear. "Okay! Call your dog off!"

"He's going to stay right where he is," Michael said, panting as he approached them, "and so are you until I say so. Put your hands on the back of your head and interlace your fingers."

"Oh man," Presley whined. "I didn't do anything!"

"Put your hands on top of your head and interlace your fingers!" Michael commanded again. "Do I need to have Turk take you down?"

"Okay, okay," Presley said, putting his hands behind his head. "Okay, just don't let him hurt me."

"You stay right where you are, and Turk will leave you alone," Faith said. "You just stay right where you are."

Michael holstered his weapon and walked behind Presley. He grabbed his left hand and placed it behind his back, cuffing it, then repeating the process on the right side.

"Am I going to jail?" Presley asked, weeping.

"We'll let you know," Michael said. "Right now, we're going to talk to you, and depending on what we hear, we'll decide if you're going to jail."

"Oh man," Presley whined. "I didn't do anything."

"So we've heard," Michael said. "Walk with me."

***

"You need to start talking to us, Leon," Michael said. "You need to give us a reason to believe you aren't responsible for these murders."

They sat in one of the smaller break rooms similar to the one where they interrogated Schoenmaker. Presley sat slumped over a table with his hands cuffed behind the chair. Turk stood and growled softly at him while Faith stood next to Turk, her face stony.

"Man, I already told you," Presley said. "I didn't do anything."

"That's not gonna cut it, Leon," Michael said. "See, we already know you did something."

Presley's eyes snapped up to him in shock. "What?"

Michael lifted a small baggie containing a dozen or so white pills. "See these? A few of your coworkers found these on the ground after you threw them down to escape us. Now, I'm not a pharmacist, but I'll bet my next paycheck that when the results come back from the lab, we're going to learn that these are prescription opiates. My guess based on the size and shape would be Norco. Pretty potent stuff. Safer than heroin and more easily obtained. I'm guessing the middle-class yuppies who take a piss next to you love the chance at a drug they can carry without risking their fluffy little careers. How much of this you sell?"

"I ain't talking without a lawyer," Presley said, lip jutting out.

"Sure," Michael said, "we can do that. If you go that way, though, then we're officially placing you under arrest for possession with intent to distribute. A little birdie tells me that this will be your third strike. A much bigger birdie tells me that three strikes in your case means ten years minimum."

Presley whined and tears formed in his eyes.

"Now on the other hand," Michael said, "you talk to me and maybe we don't tell anyone about these pills. Maybe you go on your merry way. Of course, that's only the case if you're not a murderer. If we find out you killed McIlhenny and Richardson, you're going down. I won't lie to you about that. But if you didn't kill them, and you make my life easier by sharing information that could clear you, then maybe we let you go with a warning not to fuck up again."

"You can do that?" Presley asked.

"Sure," Michael said, "we're FBI. We outrank the police."

Presley took a deep breath and said, "Can I have some water, please?"

"Sure thing," Michael said. "Faith, would you mind getting our friend here some water?"

"Absolutely," Faith said with a hard smile. "Still or sparkling?"

"What?"

"Nevermind. I'll get you some of that nice spring water from the vending machine."

"Okay," Presley said, "Um, thank you."

“Not a problem,” Faith replied with the same hard smile.

She fetched the water, returning just in time to catch Turk baring his teeth, and Presley shrank back.

“Guess he doesn’t like you,” Michael said. “Too bad.”

“He’s not gonna hurt me, is he?” Presley asked, his voice a squeak.

“Not as long as you stay right where you are,” Michael said.

“I ain’t moving,” Presley said, keeping his eyes on Turk.

Faith returned a moment later with a water bottle. She handed it to Presley, who drank greedily.

“So,” Michael said, “can you tell me where you were when Chester McIlhenny was killed?”

“Dunno,” he said. “When was he killed?”

“March 13,” Michael said. “Monday.”

“I was working Monday,” he said. “Same restroom.”

“Did anyone approach you in regard to your other business?” Michael asked.

Presley reached up and scratched his head. “Man, I can’t tell you that,” he whined. “If I rat on people, I could lose my business.”

“One might advise you to lose your business anyway,” Faith said drily.

Presley shrugged. “Man, you know how it is. I make minimum wage handing people paper towels. Half of them don’t even wash their hands and none of them tip. I have rent to pay, you know? Bills and food and—”

“Yeah, we get it,” Michael said, “but you need to answer our questions anyway.”

Presley sighed. “Yeah, a few.”

“Did you recognize any of them?”

“Of course, I recognized them, man. I don’t sell to people I don’t know. That’s a good way to get caught.”

“And look where you are now,” Faith said.

Presley met her yes. “There’s worse places to be.”

Faith nodded. “Fair enough.”

“Who did you sell to on Monday?”

“Man, I already told you. I can’t tell you.”

“And I already told you. You’re looking at being charged with murder, Leon. You’re looking real good. Now, let’s say we’re wrong and you get off the murder charge. You think the prosecution is going to let you off the hook for drugs too?”

Presley hung his head and sniffled. "Yeah, okay," he said softly. "Um, there was Betty. I don't know for sure if that's her real name, that's just the name she gives me."

"Besides Betty, who else?"

"Um, there's Rodney, Aroldis, and Fern."

"Aroldis is a male or female?"

"Male."

"Great. So, two women and two men. Can you describe the men?"

"Um, they're average, I guess. Aroldis is shorter and skinny. Rodney is tall and a little thicker. They're um … I guess forty-something?"

"You guess?"

"Man, I don't know. I don't fucking card them."

"Okay, so forty-something and average. What about on Wednesday? Working then?"

"Yeah, I was."

"Wonderful. Who did you talk to on Wednesday?"

"Just Carter," he said.

"Carter. Tell me about Carter."

"Carter's a grad student," Presley said. "He stops by once a week. Wednesday's his day."

Michael and Faith shared a glance. "Okay, we're going to show you some pictures," Michael said, "and you need to tell me if you recognize these men. Sound good?"

Presley nodded. Michael didn't expect Presley to admit to recognizing them, but Faith was excellent at reading people. If Presley was lying, she would know.

Faith watched closely as Michael showed Presley a picture of Chester McIlhenny. Presley looked him up and down and shrugged. "Looks like an old white man to me. I might have seen him, but if I did, I didn't notice him."

Michael put Chester's picture away and showed a picture of Everett Richardson. Presley peered closely. "Huh," he said, "that one looks familiar. Yeah. Yeah, he bumped into me and knocked me back into the wall. I told him 'Hey, what's up, man?' and he didn't even look my way. Rude asshole."

"Yeah? That make you want to get back at him?" Michael asked. "Maybe teach him a lesson about politeness?"

He shook his head. "No man, I didn't think about it. I mean, I remember him because he bumped into me, but most people are rude.

Maybe they don't mean to be, but you know, I'm nobody to them. I'm just the guy who holds paper towels. People don't think about me, you know."

"Yeah," Michael said. "I get that. Sit tight for a minute. Turk, watch him."

Presley shrank back slightly as Turk bared his teeth again. Faith and Michael stepped outside. As soon as the door closed, Michael said, "So? What do you think?"

Faith shook her head. "It's not him. He showed no sign of guilt or fear when he recognized Richardson. None of the glee you would expect if he had killed him either. Just mild irritation at his rudeness. He didn't recognize McIlhenny at all."

"Yeah, I figured," Michael said. "Well, we'll see if maybe he saw the killer."

They walked inside, and Michael said, "One last question, Mr. Presley. Did you notice anyone behaving unusually on either Monday or Wednesday? Especially anyone following either of the men in the pictures we showed you?"

"No, nothing like that," he said, shaking his head. "Nothing like that. People are …" he shrugged, "… just people."

Michael nodded. "All right. Thank you, Mr. Presley. I think we're done here."

"You gonna let me go?"

Michael sighed. "Yeah, I'll let you go. Don't make this mistake again, Leon. I get that times are tough, but this isn't the answer. I catch you selling drugs here again, and you strike out, you hear me?"

"Yes, sir," Leon said instantly, bobbing his head up and down. "Yes, sir, I promise, no more drugs."

Presley tiptoed slowly around Turk, who watched him impassively. As soon as he was clear, he rushed out of the room.

When he was gone, Faith turned to Michael. "You think he'll keep his promise?"

Michael shrugged and stood, heading out of the room.

"Where are you going?" Faith asked.

"I'm getting a coffee," Michael said. "You want one?"

"I thought you were cutting back," Faith said.

"Yeah, well," Michael said, walking away.

He didn't finish the thought. If he had, it would have gone something like, *yeah, well, once more, we've found a dead end and learned nothing we didn't already know. Once more, our killer is free to murder someone else, and we have to sift through hundreds more people who could be responsible. Once more, Turk sniffed out a killer only to find he wasn't a killer after all.*

"And once more, my partner is going to insist on every excuse for Turk and treat me like the asshole," he said under his breath.

Michael took another deep breath and shook his head. Leon Presley was about the most unremarkable suspect he'd ever interrogated. It was almost as though he was designed to be invisible. How do you find a killer whose only trait is being unremarkable? How do you find an unremarkable person in a sea of unremarkable people?

"Like finding a particular needle in a stack of needles," he said to himself.

It was going to be another long night.

CHAPTER SEVENTEEN

He was starting to think he really was invisible. This morning at the staff meeting, he had raised his hand and asked if they were still going to use a lottery for vacation time. He had asked twice, and Derek, the janitorial manager, hadn't even looked his way.

He had been run into three times this morning, and the people who ran into him didn't even turn to see what or who they had hit. He himself had bumped into a woman, but when he apologized, the woman passed him to run after her kids without seeming to realize she'd been nearly knocked off her feet.

If he really was invisible, *l'homme que tu ne peux pas voir,* then it would make his work that much easier. It would take away the hassle of needing to wait for cover and a lull in traffic. It would take away the haste with which he had to work, the haste that meant he might make mistakes, like he did with the second victim.

If he could take his time and focus on the victim without needing to fear getting caught, well then, he would be home free.

He walked behind his target, pushing the cart slowly but rapidly enough that he gained slowly on his prey. He smiled at a girl of about eleven or twelve who didn't notice him. *Good,* he thought. *Very good.* He really was invisible.

As he passed the girl, he pulled the needle from the cart and pushed it up his sleeve, taking care to keep the point of the needle just past his fingertips. He pushed his cart until he was only a few feet from the quarry. He pushed the cart behind a bench, leaving it there and making as though he was going to clean the bench.

He glanced around. No one was looking.

He stepped forward and with a swift movement jabbed the needle into the neck of the target. She gasped and scratched at her neck, perhaps wondering if a bee had made it underground and stung her.

The poison worked quickly. He slipped his arm around her, and she didn't even realize it happened. She slumped down, and he felt his heartbeat quicken as hers slowed.

By the time he lowered her onto the bench, she was dead.

He stood and looked around, walking slowly back to his cart. No one even glanced his direction. No one noticed that the older woman sitting with her head slumped onto her chest on the bench wasn't napping but was dead, asleep forever, not for a minute.

He looked around, and a wide grin spread across his face. He was truly invisible. Unnoticeable.

He wondered how long it would be before anyone noticed his latest kill. He found it didn't matter so much to him anymore.

CHAPTER EIGHTEEN

Faith stood outside of the break room, arms crossed. A few maintenance workers wandered over, chatting about some new video sharing app. They looked at Faith, and her expression was enough to convince them to look for another break room.

Another dead end. Faith should be used to this by now. After all, Faith often told Michael that investigative work was a whole lot of very little and then everything all at once. This was no different from any of the other cases they had solved.

Still, Faith felt the looming threat of another murder hang over her like a dark cloud. Nearly ten years with the bureau and that had never gotten easier.

And Michael was once more pissed with her. It seemed like he'd been pissed at her for almost a year straight.

It was Ellie. It all came down to Ellie.

She didn't blame Ellie directly. Whatever Ellie's faults, she didn't seem the type to sow discord between the two of them. She even seemed to genuinely want Faith to like her.

Still, ever since she had arrived, Michael had been growing more and more distant. He couldn't accept that Faith didn't love her as much as he did. Faith wasn't sure if that was because he also suspected her of being dishonest with him, or if he genuinely hated that Faith wasn't head over heels with her, but either way, Faith could see their friendship ending soon.

If it hadn't already.

She had been around long enough to see partners split. She had seen them grow to resent each other, then to hate each other, then to despise each other, then to settle into a resigned contempt that lasted long after one or both of them retired.

She never suspected that would happen with Michael. Even when they broke up, and she was afraid that the loss of their romantic relationship would drive a rift between them, she never imagined their friendship would end.

Now, it seemed it was ending like most things ended. A lot of very little and then everything all at once. When Michael returned with his coffee, Faith said, "We need to go back and look at the cameras. We need to widen the search and check footage from the entrance to the ticketing booth to the waiting area—"

"We did that, Faith, remember? There's no coverage anywhere, and where there is, there's nothing useful."

"We said that earlier, but when we looked again, we found Presley."

Michael scoffed. "Right. Presley. Yet another dead end. Hey, but we managed to force a few junkies to find another dealer. Yay us."

Faith sighed. "Michael, what do you want me to do? You want me to give up? You want me to grouse bitterly about how frustrating everything is?"

"It'd be better than not talking to me at all."

"I am talking to you!" she cried. "I tried to talk to you, and you shot me down."

"Shot you down? Why? Because I didn't immediately and enthusiastically agree with your suggestions?"

"There's a difference between a civilized discussion and scoffing, Michael."

"Yeah, there is," Michael said. "Just like there's a difference between a civilized discussion and turning into a block of ice."

"Oh, I see. I should be warm and bubbly and sweet all the time, just like your girlfriend."

She knew that was a mistake the moment she said it. Michael's eyes narrowed, and his jaw tightened. She sighed and said, "Michael, I'm sorry. I shouldn't have said that. I just—"

"No, it's fine," Michael interrupted. "Really. You're right, she's my girlfriend, not yours. You don't have to like her."

"It's not that," Faith said, "It's just … I …"

"Faith," Michael said, rubbing the bridge of his nose, "you got your wish, okay? I don't want to talk about it. In fact, let's go back to not talking at all. Turns out talking is worse."

Faith felt as though a knife were driven into her chest. She turned away from him and crossed her arms more tightly. Turk looked between the two of them and whined. Faith couldn't bring herself to look at him.

Michael finished his coffee and said, "I'm going to run to the precinct and brainstorm with Rameses. Maybe the cops have figured something out we haven't. You want to come?"

“I’ll stay here,” Faith said. “I need to look through some more security footage.”

“Suit yourself,” Michael said.

He tossed his coffee into a nearby trash can and started away, leaving Faith alone with Turk. She waited ten minutes, then led Turk away. She passed another cluster of maintenance workers on her way out, but like the previous group, they gave her a wide berth.

She headed to the ground floor to the Chinese food place they ate at the other day. She ate mechanically, the food once more not providing anything more than calories.

Normally, these moments of quiet centered her, clearing her thoughts and allowing her to separate and organize the little threads of clues that bounced around her mind. She had solved several cases this way, but this time, her mind was blank and fuzzy, like the static from a TV.

She was so out of it that when her phone rang, she jumped. The number on the phone did little to encourage her.

She took a deep breath, then answered. “Bold.”

“Is Prince there with you?” the Boss said.

Faith frowned. The Boss’s voice was different this time—quiet, almost clipped.

“No, just me,” she said, “he … stepped away for a moment.”

“Good,” the Boss said. “You don’t want him to hear this.”

Her blood froze in her chest. “What’s going on?” she asked.

“Special Agent Bold, have you been investigating the copycat Donkey Killer case?”

The ice in her veins spread through her from head to toe. “I … um …” She sighed and said, “I’ve done some snooping, yes.”

“You’ve done more than some snooping,” the Boss said, his tone still clipped. “You have, according to Special Agent Clark, identified and interrogated a suspect, attempted to question the coroner who processed one of the victims, and attempted to interrogate the family of said victim. This, in addition to stealing both physical and digital copies of the case files and reaching out by phone to multiple other people of interest. You’ve also visited crime scenes and local police forces and claimed to be an active investigator on the case.”

Faith didn’t say anything. A pit formed in her stomach and rapidly grew to a stone.

“All this,” the Boss continued, “despite being warned repeatedly by me to stay away from the case. Despite being warned repeatedly by

Clark to stay off the case. Despite, I have to add, the fact that Clark has repeatedly gone to bat for you. Not three days ago, he was defending your right to remain on this case. He's still defending it. In fact, the only reason you're not on your way back to Philly right now is that he believes that you still are the right person for the job. He respects you, Faith. You can't show him the same courtesy?"

Faith took a breath. "It's not that I don't respect him, Boss. I do. I just …"

"You just what, Bold?" the Boss shouted, his calm broken. "You just don't trust him to solve your pet case?"

"Boss, I should be the one on that case!" Faith shouted.

A few of the other diners glanced at her in alarm. She lowered her voice and said, "That case has gone nowhere, Boss. No disrespect to Clark, but it's dead end after dead end after yet another victim cut up and left for us to find."

"And how exactly have you helped, Bold? Hmm? Let's see, you terrorized a small-time drug dealer who was utterly unconnected to the case; you've talked to a whole lot of people and learned a lot of things we already know; and here's my favorite part: every lead you've pursued, you've gained from Clark's and Desrouleaux's files. You've actually followed *their leads* and relearned information they've already deduced. They dismissed Greenwood weeks before you went after him. They even managed to do it without literally breaking his door down and menacing him. But that wasn't enough for you, Bold, because you can't handle the thought that someone else would bring the copycat in. This isn't about the case, Bold. This isn't about stopping the killer before he takes another victim. This is personal, Bold. This is revenge. You've never overcome the fact that Prince had to save you from Trammell, that you couldn't beat him yourself, so now you want to beat his mimic so you can convince yourself that you're an untouchable badass."

"That's not …" she stopped before she finished the sentence. Deep down, Faith knew that what the Boss said had a lot of truth to it. She sat glumly as the Boss finished his diatribe.

"Bold, I want Prince to take lead on this case. You are to do as he says without argument or question."

Faith stiffened, "Boss, I—"

"I swear to God, Bold, if I hear your voice again other than to say yes sir after I instruct you to say yes sir, I will drive to New York personally and take your badge and gun."

Faith pressed her lips together. The Boss waited for ten seconds before continuing. "Wonderful. You are to do as Special Agent Prince says without argument or question. He will take lead on this case effective immediately. When you return to Philadelphia, your first stop will be my office. You understand? You better come in smelling like day-old sweat, Bold, because if you so much as stop home to shower, I'll take your badge and gun from you. Your K9 unit too."

Faith stiffened again and whipped her eyes to Turk. After over a year with Turk, it was easy to forget that he wasn't actually her pet but the property of the Bureau. But he wasn't. Maybe in name he was, but he was her companion, the closest thing she had left to a friend. Even her connection with David wasn't as strong as her connection with Turk. She couldn't lose him.

"When you arrive, you and I will discuss your future with the Bureau," the Boss continued. "Is all of this clear? You can say yes sir now."

"Yes, sir," Faith said quietly.

"Outstanding. I'm calling Prince right now just in case you're deciding to lie to me again. Goodbye, Bold."

He hung up. Faith sat where she was for several minutes, staring straight ahead. Her food remained untouched and eventually cooled. A busser approached cautiously, motioning to ask Faith if he should clear the table. She didn't respond, and he moved on.

Turk laid his head on her lap and looked sympathetically into her eyes, but he brought no comfort to Faith considering she might soon lose him.

After a while, she managed to stand. Her phone buzzed, a text from Michael. *Just talked to the Boss. I'm sorry, Faith.*

She put her phone back in her pocket without responding and headed back inside the terminal. She walked for a few minutes before sitting at a bench on a platform a few removed from the scene of the two murders. She stared ahead as a train pulled to a stop and unloaded several hundred passengers while several hundred more boarded. They milled around Faith without giving her or Turk a second glance or even a first glance for that matter.

She had seen this coming. She knew it was only a matter of time. She had just managed to convince herself that somehow what she knew would happen wouldn't actually happen.

She realized how foolish she was now. Of course, she would be caught. She couldn't expect to interfere in an active investigation without the agents assigned to the case noticing her interference. Of course, they would learn of her involvement.

Of course, she had convinced herself that when they did catch her, she'd have a wealth of new information to share. Instead, as the Boss had brutally pointed out, she had learned nothing that they didn't already know.

Her heart sank further as she realized they were right. The Boss, Michael, Clark, Doctor West—they were all right about her. She had never left that barn. She still sat in that chair, hands and feet bound, screaming in agony and fear and most of all humiliation as Jethro Trammell cut through her knees and ankles and wrists straight through to her soul. Trammell was dead and gone, and her physical wounds had healed, but her mind remained rooted to the moment where she realized in the most terrible way possible just how utterly helpless she was.

And now her failure was finally complete. Jethro had beaten her after all. It had just taken her a little longer to die than the others.

Let's see how you bleed, little girl, he'd said to her.

"Very little, and then all at once," she whispered under her breath.

CHAPTER NINETEEN

Faith stared ahead at the crowd. Another train stopped, and she watched as a stressed-looking, middle-aged man with a briefcase shouldered his way past a younger man and an elderly woman, nearly knocking the woman to the ground. Not only did the man with the briefcase move on without so much as a backwards glance, but the younger man ignored the elderly woman, glaring and lifting a finger at the older man before nearly colliding with her himself.

No one cared. No one cared that no one cared. Everyone was too busy with their own lives to care that their actions affected others. Like the thousands of people who walked right by Chester McIlhenny's dead body without even realizing he was dead or even there in the first place. Like the hundreds who fought with police so they could snap a picture of Everett Richardson's dead body and post it on their social media pages without regard for the fact that he was a living, breathing human like they were only hours ago.

She watched people continue to jostle and push and fight their way past others, watched as they ignored the panhandlers and janitors and maintenance workers and wondered how a species so utterly dependent on social interaction could treat others so callously.

Then again, McIlhenny and Richardson were no saints. She thought of Blake Richardson's words about his brother, that other people didn't seem to matter much to him. There was a cruel irony in the fact that he and McIlhenny were treated in their deaths as callously as they treated others in life. The killer no doubt enjoyed knowing that.

The answer hit Faith so hard that she actually gasped. Turk instantly jumped to his feet and looked around, trying to identify what had threatened her. She reached down and scratched absently behind his ears, mind racing.

The killer watched. He watched them after he staged them. He watched them so he could see people ignoring them the way they ignored him. Those crowds that gathered around the bodies camouflaged him, allowed him to watch without being noticed.

So, the killer was an employee who was personally insulted by the victims. He killed them, left their bodies, and watched while thousands of people passed them by. He watched them when they were discovered and watched as everyone treated them the same way he believed they treated him.

But which of the employees could be the killer? She had seen several of them, dozens of them, in fact, gathered around Richardson's body. All of them seemed to be as morbidly fascinated as the passengers. She recalled the janitor she had seen watching the commotion around Richardson's body the other day. He could be the killer but so could any of the other janitors, maintenance workers, bathroom attendants, and ticket-takers that also gathered around.

They were on the right track. The killer was an employee, but it would take weeks, possibly months to investigate and rule out everyone who wasn't the killer—weeks or months for him to figure out an exit plan. They could arrange to sit in on exit interviews, but they couldn't do anything about the people who just left with no notice, a common occurrence at any low-wage job.

They needed to find him soon, before the noose tightened to the point that they scared him off.

She stood and led Turk back into the building. She headed to the security office, and when she arrived, the desk officer sighed heavily and said, "Do you want me to just email you the footage? I can't keep giving up my seat so you guys can watch the same footage over and over. For God's sake, it's like you want him to get away with another murder."

Faith didn't have time to argue with him or to feel offended. "Move over," she said, flashing her ID, "you can file a complaint later if you want."

He heaved another sigh, then slowly got up from the chair and sidled out of the room. Faith sat and quickly pulled up footage from the day Chester McIlhenny was killed. She identified a janitor picking up trash near where Chester sat, the world oblivious to the fact that he was dead. She watched him, but he showed no special interest in Chester and moved on after cleaning the area around the bench.

He returned to the platform several more times, but so did two other janitors. A ticketing booth sat at the corner of the frame, staffed by the same three ticket-takers. Two maintenance workers checked an electrical panel nearby, probably preparing for the launch of twenty-four-hour service that night. That was eight suspects already. Of those eight, the three janitors and the three ticket-takers remained when Kylie Bonaparte screamed as Chester's body rolled forward off the bench.

The footage of Richardson's death revealed a similar issue. There were over two dozen employees among the crowd of hundreds this time, nine of which had remained in the area throughout Richardson's brief tenure as an unknown dead body. Five of those nine were among the six that worked the platform the day Chester died.

And that was only what the camera picked up. Who knew what the camera had missed? Richardson's body wasn't even on camera. All Faith could see was the crowd that gathered around it. If Faith's experience was indicative of a typical day, there were at least a dozen other employees who would have spent the workday in the area out of view of the camera.

Well, they could start with these five. It was at least somewhat likely the killer was among them. She could only hope that if he was, the killer would be spooked into revealing his identity.

That was a slim hope indeed.

She called the security officer back inside. "Should I expect you to interrupt my workday again?" he asked, irritated.

"No," she said, "not unless we find another body."

"Well, if you do, I hope this one leads you to the killer," he said, "so you can finally get out of my hair."

Faith's lips thinned. "I wonder how many people will think so little of you if you end up being the body we find," she said.

"Almost everyone," the security officer said without missing a beat.

He sat in his chair and resumed his stoic monitoring of the cameras, pointedly ignoring Faith. After a moment, she left the room, Turk on her heels.

She didn't wish for a dead body, of course, but it seemed that their only chance of finding the killer would be to be present at another scene and happen to catch him staring. She couldn't accept that as their only option.

As with so many things lately, what Faith could or couldn't accept didn't matter. Faith walked perhaps thirty yards from the office when Turk suddenly stopped, lifting his nose.

"What do you smell, boy?" Faith asked. "What do you smell?"

Turk whined and put his nose to the ground. He began to trot, following the scent. Faith kept pace with him, scanning the platform for anything suspicious. Faith followed him across three more platforms, checking the crowds of passengers for anyone behaving strangely or for anyone sitting or standing in a strange position. No one appeared to be sleeping or even sitting still. It was the start of the afternoon rush, and passengers milled about everywhere in their haste to board their connecting train or reach the line of buses and cabs waiting outside.

Turk picked up the pace as they reached a fourth platform, moving quicker as he approached the source of the smell. People jostled Faith as she hurried to keep up, occasionally offering a miffed, "Watch it!" or "Out of my way!" but mostly ignoring her.

Turk stopped in front of a bench upon which sat a woman in her late forties. The woman's chin rested on her chest, and she slumped forward slightly, eyes closed.

Faith sighed when she reached the body, for body was what it certainly was. She reached forward and checked for a pulse. She wasn't surprised to find there wasn't one.

She looked around quickly to see if anyone was watching the scene, but with the crowd milling around heavily, she couldn't pick out any one individual who might be watching instead of moving. She pulled her phone from her pocket and called Michael.

"Hey, Faith," he said in a tired voice. "How are you?"

"Nevermind that right now," Faith said. "Where are you?"

"I'm grabbing lunch," he said, "by the precinct. I … I needed some space."

Faith sighed. "Well, I can understand that, but it'll have to wait. We have a third victim."

"Shit," Michael said, "I'm on my way. See if you can keep the vultures off for now."

"Will do," she said.

She hung up and looked around, but no one had yet taken notice of the lone FBI agent and her K9 standing in front of a woman who was not merely sleeping. She decided the best way to keep the vultures at bay was to simply remain quiet. She sat on the bench next to the body and continued to scan the crowd for signs of anyone looking their way.

No one looked.

***

The police arrived first, three minutes after Faith hung up. They reached the scene and immediately began to cordon the area off. Faith counted eight officers. Six of them wore riot gear, complete with batons and shields. Of the two that weren't wearing riot gear, one cordoned off the bench while the other—a sergeant—approached Faith.

He wasn't the only one to approach. One woman and a dog may have been invisible to the crowd, but a full squad of police in riot gear was another thing entirely. Before the approaching sergeant could reach Faith, someone screamed. Another person—a young man of maybe nineteen or twenty wearing a sweater emblazoned with the flaming torch logo of New York University—called, "Hey! They found another body on the subway!"

"Goddammit," the sergeant muttered.

Chaos ensued after that. The crowd around the bench first receded, melting away in shock as people panicked and scanned for signs of danger, then collapsed on them like a tsunami.

"Disperse that crowd!" the sergeant shouted.

"No!" Faith called. "Keep them away from the bench but don't clear the platform!"

The sergeant turned to her incredulously. "Are you serious?" he said. "What the hell are you doing? There's only eight of us right now!"

"Do you have more officers on the way?" Faith asked.

"Yeah," he said. "Another dozen riot officers plus whoever Detective Rameses is bringing with him."

"How long before the riot squad gets here?" Faith asked.

"Fifteen minutes, at least."

"Good," Faith said. "Your job is to keep the crowd away from this bench—and *only* this bench—for those fifteen minutes. Anyone who respects the cordon is to be left alone, do you understand?"

No sooner had Faith said that than the man in the NYU sweater rushed the riot officers. He launched himself into one of the officers, phone outstretched, clicking madly until the officer threw him backwards. One of the other officers drew his baton, but the sergeant shouted, "Keep your weapon at your side, Jenkins!"

The officer snapped his head to affix his sergeant with the same incredulous look the sergeant gave Faith a moment ago. "Are you kidding?" he asked. "There's hundreds of them, Sarge!"

Faith looked around and saw that he was right. The crowd had grown swiftly, quickly filling the platform and spreading to the neighboring platforms. Security officers began to converge, and Faith flagged them down. They made their way slowly through the rapidly energizing crowd, and when they reached within earshot, Faith cupped her hand over her mouth and shouted, "Help the police maintain the perimeter!"

They nodded and expanded the circle of officers protecting the bench. With the reinforcements, the sergeant was able to talk to Faith again. "Who noticed the body?"

"My K9 smelled her," Faith said, continuing to scan the crowd.

"He smelled her?" The sergeant turned toward the slumped woman and sniffed gingerly. "I don't smell anything."

Faith didn't bother trying to tell him that a dog's sense of smell was many times more sensitive than his own. She continued to look around, but there was no way of knowing which of the employees that gawked along with the rest of the crowd might be the killer, if any of them were.

"Dammit," she whispered under her breath.

There were just too many people. She couldn't hope to spot one person from a crowd this size.

The sergeant returned to her and asked, "Did you find any ID on her?"

"No, I haven't examined the body yet," she said. "I wanted to keep from alerting the crowd."

A trace of frustration must have crept into her voice when she said that because the sergeant immediately went on the defensive. "Well, I'm sorry, ma'am. Detective Rameses called me and told me to get my ass here with some riot officers ASAP. Said your partner told him you had found another body and needed help right away."

"I needed *his* help right away," Faith griped, mostly to herself.

"You want us to leave?" the sergeant groused irritably.

"No," Faith said. "You can check for ID but leave the rest of the examination for CSI."

"Yes ma'am," he jibed.

He left to check for ID while Faith continued to scan the crowd. "Where are you?" she whispered.

They had to find him this time. If they didn't, they would be out of luck again until there was another body.

CHAPTER TWENTY

Faith scanned the crowd, mind racing. She counted eight employees in all: three janitors, a maintenance worker, and four other people in nondescript uniforms who could have been concierges or ticket-takers. They all regarded the scene with the same frenzied excitement as everyone else. Faith watched their movements and facial expressions closely, but from this distance, it was impossible to pick up on any signs of guilt, if there were any to pick up on.

"Anita Barkley," the sergeant said, "forty-eight, five-foot-ten and … well, the ID says 180 pounds, but I'll bet my lunch she was closer to 280."

Faith rolled her eyes and asked, more to keep the sergeant busy than anything else, "Can you run her ID and see if she had a record?"

"Sure," he said. "I assume you mean besides the record for most doughnuts consumed in a twenty-four-hour period."

Faith ignored that gem as well. Turk had caught a scent. He stood, ears pricked, staring intently into the crowd.

Faith followed his eyes. "What is it? What do you see, boy?"

Turk barked once, causing the front row of the crowd to recoil. The riot officers stumbled forward, then nearly fell backward when the crowd resurged again.

"What do you see, boy?" Faith repeated, staring at the crowd ahead of Turk. "Where is he?"

Turk barked again, and Faith saw him this time. A man dressed in the gray coveralls and scuffed boots of a maintenance worker. A tool vest hung over his shoulders, and his face wore an expression that reminded Faith of someone watching a prize fight—a mixture of horror and excitement. His gaze landed on Turk's and fear first joined, then banished the other two emotions.

He began to back away slowly, eyes fixed on Turk. Faith started to follow, Turk at her side. "Hey!" she called. "Stop!"

At the sound of her voice, the man's eyes snapped up to hers. He grinned, a look of fear and not mirth, and turned, disappearing into the crowd.

"Dammit!" Faith cried. "Go get him, boy!"

Turk lunged into the crowd, weaving easily through the crammed onlookers. Faith tried to keep up, calling, "FBI! Clear the way!" but the people, excited almost to a frenzy by the sight of a body and a rapidly more aggressive police blockade, didn't notice her until she was right on top of them, and she quickly fell behind Turk and the maintenance worker as she shoved and pushed her way through.

She heard Turk bark and called, "Get him, boy! Take him down!"

In the back of her head, she recalled the Boss's irate response the last time she let Turk chase a suspect, but she dismissed that concern immediately. There was a dead body thirty feet behind her, and she would be damned if she allowed another one. If she happened to scare someone who wasn't the real killer, so be it. If that happened to get back to the Boss, and she was responsible for another complaint against the Bureau, so be that as well. She was probably fired when she got back to Philadelphia anyway. At least she could bring one last killer to justice before she was demoted to civilian and forced to work as a private investigator or security officer like the other failed special agents she'd known over the years.

Turk barked again, more distantly this time, and Faith cursed again under her breath. She wondered if she should call Turk to wait for her. She didn't want the killer—if he was the killer—to lead him toward the tracks and throw him off of the platform the way Schoenmaker had. Turk had survived that brush with death, but she knew chances were slim he'd get that lucky again.

Then again, she didn't want to lose her suspect. If he was the killer and he got away yet again, he might be spooked into ceasing his spree and leaving the Terminal entirely. With the little evidence they had, none of it leading to a particular individual, chances were slim to none that they would ever apprehend him. Faith could live with that if she could believe that he would be cowed into stopping his murderous ways for good, but deep down, she thought that he would only be scared for a while before the urge would grow too strong, and he would strike again, maybe in a different place in a different city. Other killers had followed the same pattern, killing until the heat grew too great for them, then hiding only to resurface when things cooled down.

"Turk!" she called. "Turk, where are you!"

She received an answering bark and was somewhat comforted to note it seemed no farther away than before, albeit no closer. "Good boy!" she called. "Go get him! For Pete's sake, *clear a path!"*

Her shout caused the crowd in front of her to momentarily give way, and she caught sight of Turk, about forty yards ahead, still chasing the maintenance worker, who was now running full tilt, barreling through the onlookers and pushing several to the ground in his haste to escape.

Faith sprinted after him, shouting, "FBI! Stop!"

He didn't stop, of course. He turned, and when he saw Turk gaining on him, he cried out and began running even faster. Faith tried a new tactic. "Stop, or I'll tell him to bite!"

The maintenance worker turned around in alarm, this time meeting Faith's eyes. "I swear to God, I'll tell him to bite you!" Faith said. "Stop running!"

They were on the outskirts of the crowd now, and several passengers, unaware of the chaos unfolding at the adjacent platform, turned to her in alarm when she said that. The maintenance employee turned away from Faith, scanning for an exit, but the momentary hesitation allowed Turk to reach him, and when he turned to see the big German shepherd snarling at him, he released a scream that sounded exactly like an "EEP!" from an old cartoon and fell to the ground, hands in front of him to ward Turk off.

Turk, ever the professional, stopped just in front of him, growling and barking but not snapping or biting at the downed quarry.

"Please!" the man shrieked. "Don't let him eat me!"

Faith blinked, surprised at the absurdity of the demand. She quickly regained her composure, however, and said, "Turk, heel."

Turk immediately calmed and returned to her side. The maintenance worker stared wide-eyed at Faith, rooted to the spot.

"You and I are going to have a little chat," Faith said.

"Please," the man whispered. "Don't let him kill me!"

Faith sighed. "He's not going to kill you. You talk to me, and he won't even touch you. What's your name?"

"Ernesto," he said in the same keening whisper.

"Nice to meet you, Ernesto," Faith said. "I'm Special Agent Faith Bold. What were you doing on that platform?"

"I was on my lunch break," he said. "I was working on some of the grounded locomotives on 7G and decided to head to the Italian place on 9E for some pasta. They have good ravioli."

He remained on his back with his hands splayed out in front of him, and Faith said, "You can stand, Ernesto, just don't start running, or Turk *will* take you down."

"No, no, no running," he said, slowly getting to his feet, one hand extended fully in front of him in a warding-off gesture. "No running."

"So, you were on your lunch break," Faith said, "and you had to cross several platforms, including the one where a dead woman sat unnoticed on a bench, because you just had to have your ravioli."

"Please," he whispered, "I didn't know there was a dead woman on that platform. I just saw the crowd and stopped to see what everyone was looking at."

"Hmm," Faith said, "ever use phenol, Ernesto?"

"Phenol?" he said, brow furrowing. "Is that a drug? I don't do drugs, ma'am. Not since my aunt OD'ed on heroin six years ago. I threw out all my marijuana. I don't even drink anymore. You can …" He took a deep breath and lowered his arm, then stiffened. "You can have your dog search me if you need to. Just please don't let him hurt me. I'm scared of dogs. My cousin was bit by a dog when I was a kid. I'll never forget the way she screamed."

"Fun family," Faith muttered to herself. Out loud, she said, "You have my word, Ernesto. You stay still and let Turk search you, and he won't so much as lick you. Okay?"

"Okay," he said. "Okay."

He closed his eyes and grinned that wide fear-grin again, trembling like a leaf as Turk approached. Faith wasn't concerned about drugs, of course, but if Turk caught a scent of phenol, then this man might be their killer.

Already, Faith had her doubts. The man was clearly legitimately terrified of Turk. Terrified men made terrible liars, and this man was sharing some rather personal family secrets, which indicated to Faith that he was in no shape to hide anything right now.

Still, Turk *had* smelled something, and when he reached Ernesto, he immediately smelled it again, recoiling and shaking his head, pawing at his nose. Faith pursed her lips grimly. "Ernesto, what are you hiding?" she said, stepping closer.

"Nothing!" he squeaked. "I swear, nothing!"

"Try again," Faith said. "My K9 smelled something on you. Something very strong. Tell me about phenol, Ernesto. Tell me what you have."

"I don't know what phenol is," he said. "Is that …" his eyes widened. "Wait!" he cried with almost desperate excitement. "Is that in bleach? I mean, I know bleach has chlorine, but does it have phenol too?"

Faith approached closely, and when she reached him, she could smell it—a strong, astringent odor that flared her nostrils and burned her eyes. She sighed and called Turk off.

"Was it the bleach?" Ernesto asked hopefully. "Maybe that's what angered your dog?"

"Yeah," Faith said, "might be."

Once more, Turk had followed a lead, and once more, Turk had been wrong. She couldn't understand it. She had worked three cases with him, and in all three cases, he had not once been wrong. Was he losing it too?

"Yeah," Ernesto said, visibly relaxing now that Turk wasn't snapping at him. "Yeah, I thought maybe that might be it. My wife accidentally put my uniform in with the whites. That's why there's all these stains on it."

He pointed out several light blotches on the front of his coveralls and said, "I think maybe your dog smelled the bleach and the scent just angered him. I'm very sorry. I'll have it replaced, I promise."

"That's fine, Ernesto," Faith said. "You're free to go."

"I'm … are you sure?" he asked, staring fearfully at Turk. "He won't get mad again?"

"No, you're fine," Faith said. "Sorry for the confusion."

"That's okay," he said, "I'll, um … bye."

He rushed off, glancing over his shoulder a few yards away to make sure Turk wasn't following him. Faith sighed and pressed both of her hands to her temples.

What was she missing? Why would Turk be alerted by bleach? Bleach wouldn't heighten the smell of phenol, it would mask it.

It masked it.

Her eyes snapped open. A janitor. It was for sure a janitor. Pure phenol had an overwhelmingly sweet and pungent odor. Even in amounts far less than what was needed to kill a man, the smell would be unmistakable.

Unless, of course, the odor was masked by industrial strength cleaning chemicals. That would explain the false positives Turk found earlier. If what he was smelling was phenol *and* cleaning chemicals, then he could possibly be thrown off by the presence of one but not the other.

She started back toward the platform, scanning for the janitors she had seen earlier. There were several dozen janitors employed at the terminal, so there was no guarantee that her killer would be one of the one's she'd seen earlier, but if nothing else, she had narrowed their pool of suspects even further.

She caught sight of one of the janitors, standing at the very back of the crowd next to a bucket of mop water. He leaned on the mop and stared ahead at the crowd, a small smile on his lips. As Faith drew closer, she recognized him. He was the same janitor she had seen at the back of the crowd gathered around Everett Richardson's body.

Turk growled low in his throat, and Faith said, "Quiet, Turk. We're going to do this nice and easy."

She looked away from the janitor, keeping him in her peripheral as she passed him and entered the crowd. She and Turk made their way slowly through the massed throng until they were directly in front of the janitor. She allowed the crowd to slowly jostle her back until she was close to him. Then she turned and before the surprised janitor could react, she reached him.

"Good afternoon," she said. "FBI. Can I talk to you for a moment?"

CHAPTER TWENTY ONE

He really must be invisible. He had killed this woman in broad daylight and sat her on a bench mere yards from the boarding platform, and not one of the hundreds of people around had noticed him, even when he struggled to carry the portly woman to the bench and carefully positioned her.

He recalled how it used to frustrate him as a child when people ignored him. He would play hide and seek, and inevitably, the other kids wouldn't find him. They would walk right past where he was hiding, sometimes even meeting his eyes, and move on without so much as a second glance.

And now, though hundreds—or by now thousands—of people pushed and shoved almost violently past each other, none of them noticed him. They bumped and jostled him but didn't seem to realize they had hit anything. Those that did, glanced around, their eyes traveling over him but never landing on him before they moved on.

He obviously wasn't invisible all the time. After all, his supervisors could see him when they needed to assign him a task, and cars stopped for him when he crossed the street in the quiet, residential neighborhood he lived in. Still, this morning, his supervisor had called him into his office to chastise him for missing a morning meeting only to learn that he had, in fact, been at the meeting and seated in the very front row.

Perhaps his invisibility was selective. He would be visible when he needed to be and invisible when he needed to be. He lifted his hand and flexed his fingers. He could see himself clearly, but he could see himself clearly when he killed the woman now sitting behind a cordon of police and security, so that wasn't an adequate test of his power.

He turned to one of the other members of the crowd and waved his hand in front of her. She didn't so much as flinch.

"Hey!" he cried. "Hello!"

His voice was softened by the noise of the crowd but still clearly understandable. Still, the woman didn't react. He grinned widely and clapped his hands next to her ear. She waved her hand absently as though shooing a mosquito but didn't even turn his way.

He laughed and looked away from her, leaning against his mop. He briefly considered killing her, too, but he was in a great mood right now. He didn't feel a need to kill her.

He smiled and watched as the police struggled to fend off the crowd. Now they noticed. Now they saw. They had their spectacle, and his victim was finally as important and attention-worthy in death as she thought she was in life.

He scanned the crowd and found he no longer felt the same hatred toward them. It used to infuriate him how no one noticed him, how he could work there day in and day out, cleaning up other people's shit and sweat and spit and garbage, and they would treat him as no more worthy of attention than the cans where he would dump binfuls of discarded gum, wrappers, bags, bottles, cans, and occasionally even needles.

A momentary flash of anger coursed through him. Used needles! He had thrown away used needles! He could have died of any number of diseases had he ever been unlucky enough to prick himself with those needles. In fact, he *had* pricked himself with a needle once and spent several days in terror that he might come down with AIDS or some exotic as-yet-undiscovered illness thanks to some random junkie who couldn't even be bothered to dispose of his paraphernalia in one of the many clearly marked bins.

That was what prompted him to start killing. It was what had led him to choose a needle and poison to punish the transgressors he deemed worthy of punishment. He had purchased the needles from a pharmacy, pulling them off of a shelf full of syringes marketed toward those with diabetes.

The phenol had been harder to come by, but he had managed to find a chemical plant that didn't ask too many questions and purchased a fifty-five-gallon drum of the poison under a false name. That drum would last the rest of his life and possibly longer in case some other invisible agent of justice decided to pick up where he left off.

He laughed at that. Imagine. He could be the first in a long line of angels of death that patrolled the Twin Cities Terminal, ensuring that the cold, indifferent assholes of the world met the end they deserved.

Angel of Death. He liked that. He preferred it to the name the press had given him—the Subway Vampire. As though he were some menacing force of darkness rather than an agent of the light.

Then again, to those mired in darkness, daylight seemed blinding.

Wow. That was good. Perhaps when he reached an age where he could no longer reasonably carry out his work, he could enjoy a second career as a writer.

Well, there were many years of health and vitality yet. He wasn't young, but he was far from old. He would avenge himself and all the other downtrodden people of the world for decades to come. He wondered, did God grant him this power, or was he simply one of the randomly gifted individuals of the world, blessed with an ability that he could use to enact justice?

He caught sight of the FBI woman and her dog again and froze. If ever he needed to remain invisible, now was the time. This woman had come uncomfortably close to discovering him, probably would have discovered him if not for his gift.

She stared directly at him, and he remained perfectly still, gripping the mop and pressing down to keep the bucket from moving and revealing his presence. She continued to stare as she approached, no doubt wondering why a mop was standing directly upright in a bucket with no one there to hold it.

Then she spoke. "Good afternoon," she said, meeting his eyes. "FBI. Can I talk to you for a moment?"

He stared at her, frozen in shock. Was she speaking to him? Could she *see* him?

Then the dog growled low in its throat, and when he looked down and saw the deadly intent in the shepherd's eyes, he knew.

He wasn't invisible. He was only lucky.

His mind raced with panic. He had grown too cocky. He had grown arrogant, and in his arrogance, he had allowed himself to be caught.

"Sir," the agent said, her eyes narrowing. "Can I talk to you for a moment?"

Her hand drifted toward her jacket pocket, where no doubt a handgun waited.

He lifted his eyes to meet hers and cried out, throwing the mop at the agent and kicking the bucket of water over. The agent's hands snapped forward, catching the mop with lightning-fast reflexes. The dog's reflexes proved equally sharp, and he easily avoided the flying bucket, but couldn't maintain his feet in the soapy mess that spread across the ground around him. He stumbled and fell onto his rump, and the FBI agent looked toward him for a brief second.

A brief second was all he needed. He turned and sprinted away, shouting and screaming as he made his way toward the next platform.

CHAPTER TWENTY TWO

Faith looked up to see her quarry sprinting away from the crowd, shrieking as he rushed toward the next platform. She looked at Turk, who continued to struggle through the soapy mess. "Turk, follow me," she commanded.

She rushed after him, drawing her handgun and shouting, "FBI! Stop!"

He didn't stop, and after a moment, it became clear that he was outrunning her. Faith holstered her weapon and increased her pace, moving faster than she had since the Marine Corps. A twinge of pain flashed in her right knee where almost two years ago Jethro Trammell had sliced the tendons connecting her thigh to her calf. She grimaced and shook off the pain, continuing to rush after the killer, for she was sure now that this one really was the man responsible for the three deaths so far.

So far.

Her jaw set. There would not be another death.

She lowered her head, lengthened her stride, and finally began to gain on the killer, albeit slowly, very slowly. He was fast. Too fast. She wondered if he had been an athlete in a past life. Whatever he used to be, what he was now was a psychopathic killer, and she would catch him and stop him no matter what it took.

It might take everything. He rushed through three platforms and showed no sign of slowing, continuing to shriek every few seconds when he turned and saw Faith still pursuing him. Her side burned, and her knee throbbed. A few moments later, her ankles joined in, sending bolts of lightning up her legs with each footfall as she tried and failed to gain ground on him.

When they reached platform 7A, he veered suddenly to the left, heading straight for the tracks. Faith watched in alarm as he leapt onto the tracks without slowing.

She rushed to the edge, expecting to see him lying on the tracks injured or dead. Instead, she caught only a brief flash of gray coverall as he ran into the tunnel.

"Shit!" she cried.

She jumped onto the tracks, rolling when she landed. Her hand came down on the nearest rail, and she stood and rushed after him, calling once more for him to stop.

Once more, her cry was ignored. The janitor ran down the tracks, deftly avoiding the middle rail and quickly widening the distance between himself and Faith, who ran alongside the tracks and had to move more slowly to avoid tripping over the tracks.

God, it was like he was a parkour champion or something. He moved like a dancer, effortlessly placing his feet inches from the center rail while avoiding contact that would surely kill him. She rushed after him, calling for him to stop, but he continued to ignore her and ran, shrieking, down the tunnel.

Faith knew she couldn't reach him running the way she was. She took a breath, then climbed the rail onto the maintenance walkway. She didn't trust herself to walk on the tracks without stumbling into the rail.

By the time she was able to sprint at full speed again, the killer was twenty yards ahead of her. She drew her weapon and cried, "Stop! Stop, or I'll shoot!"

The janitor shrieked something unintelligible back at her and continued to run. She paused and took aim with her weapon, then once more decided against it. At this range, her chances of hitting a moving target were slim. If she did hit him, he could fall against the electrified rail and burn himself to a crisp, eliminating any chance of positively identifying him as the killer.

She holstered her weapon once more and resumed pursuit. The few seconds of delay allowed the killer to gain another fifteen yards on her, and she could barely make out his shadow every few yards under the dim glow of the tunnel's lights.

She chased him for maybe a quarter mile before reaching an unused platform. The tracks split here, one line veering to the left and continuing along the route, the other heading into the platform and ending abruptly at a stack of planks and sections of rail.

She stopped at the fork and looked down the two routes. A moment later, she saw the flash of gray coverall as the killer hoisted himself onto the platform and disappeared behind a stack of rails wrapped in plastic sheeting.

She drew her weapon and walked slowly toward the platform. "Hey!" she cried out. "Stop!"

There was no answer. The killer's shrieking stopped.

"There's nowhere for you to go!" she cried out. "There are more police and FBI on the way! Surrender yourself now, and you won't be hurt!"

The sound of laughter echoed through the platform. Faith looked around, taking stock of her surroundings. There were stacks of rails, planks, and boxes scattered around the platform, covered in plastic sheeting. Behind the barrier at the end of the tracks sat three rail cars, all in disrepair. This was either a maintenance yard or a supply depot. Maybe a dumping ground for old supplies and equipment the railroad no longer needed.

There were far too many places to hide.

Laughter echoed again, and Faith whirled around, training her weapon behind the nearest stack of boxes. She carefully walked around the boxes, stepping softly and listening.

Footfalls echoed around her, and she spun around again, looking for any sign of her prey. Or her predator.

The thought that he might be hunting her chilled her, but she pushed through it. She wasn't the same agent who had been kidnapped and tortured by Jethro Trammell, and dangerous as this maniac was, he was no Donkey Killer.

"It's over," she called out. "No more running! We *will* find you!"

"Not if they find you first!"

She spun toward the voice, finger tightening on the trigger of her handgun. Laughter echoed once more through the platform, and she cursed under her breath. Sound echoed too much for her to pinpoint its origin. She walked among the stacks and listened, but every footfall and laugh seemed to come from everywhere at once.

She decided to keep him talking. She might not be able to tell the direction the sound came from, but she could at least make a rough guess at how far away he was.

"What's the plan?" she asked. "Kill me and run? Where will you go? An awful lot of people saw you."

"No one saw me!" he cried. "I was invisible! No one but you even noticed I was there!"

"Did that upset you?" she asked. "Is that why you killed those people?"

More laughter. "Does it matter? Not to you, miss FBI! No one will see you either!"

"Listen," she said. "I can tell your story. I can make sure that people notice you. I can make sure that everyone everywhere knows your name and knows why you had to do what you did. You can be an inspiration to others like you who live life ignored by everyone around them!"

"Everyone is ignored by everyone around them," the killer's voice called, a little closer than it was before. "I thought I was truly invisible, that God had granted me a special dispensation to enact His vengeance on the uncaring assholes of the world, but you know what? Everyone is invisible because everyone is blind. Everyone sees only the world that exists directly in front of their noses and then only when something impacts them directly!"

Faith crept closer to the voice as the killer ranted. It reminded her of a game she played as a kid where one person would wear a blindfold and try to find a hidden object, following the directions of the other kids, who would shout warmer as the blindfolded kid approached the object and colder if they moved away from it.

"Listen," Faith called. "If you come with me, then people will know your story. They'll know who you are. They'll know why you did this. You'll be a legend."

The killer cackled laughter again. "I already am a legend, didn't you hear? I'm the Subway Vampire!"

Warmer.

"People fear you," she called. "They don't love you. They don't understand you. They think you're just killing for fun. They don't know your purpose."

More laughter. "No one will understand me, FBI!"

Colder.

She turned and started walking toward another pile of rails covered in plastic sheeting. The killer continued to rant. "You think I'm stupid? Well, I'm not. I might be crazy, but I'm not a fool."

Colder.

Stifling frustration, Faith changed directions again as the killer continued to rant.

"You won't call me a hero. You won't *understand*," he sneered, "and neither will anyone else. Once you have me locked away and stifled, you'll just call me a crazed killer like every other crazed killer."

Well, he's not wrong. He's also growing farther away.

Faith's annoyance rose, but she forced herself to stay calm. "You're right," she said. "I don't understand. I don't understand how you could think that killing innocent people will make a damned bit of difference.

Do you think people who read about your crimes will learn some lesson about being considerate of others?"

"Of course not!" he said. "I'm not *doing* it for other people! I'm doing it for *me!* As far as making a difference—well, in the scheme of things, I suppose I *won't* make a difference. What's a few insignificant deaths in an entire herd of people who think only of themselves?"

Still colder.

Faith looked around, wondering where else the killer could possibly be. Her eyes moved toward the abandoned railroad cars. She stopped and turned toward them, slowly walking closer, handgun trained in front of her.

"No difference, FBI! No difference at all! But a few assholes got what they deserved, and you know what? That's enough for me."

Warmer!

Faith stifled a smile as she approached the cars. "Pathetic!" she called, her voice dripping with contempt. "That's really the legacy of the Subway Vampire?" She whined dramatically as she continued, "Oh no! People are so mean to me, so I poisoned some of them like a coward to get back at them for ignoring the poor, little janitor!"

More laughter. Faith was close enough now that she could tell for sure that it was coming from behind the furthest of the abandoned cars. She walked slowly, keeping the killer talking so he wouldn't hear her approach.

"You're not a vampire," she said. "You're a snake. You hide in the grass and strike, then run away and hide."

"You're right," he said. "I'm not a vampire."

He was so close she could almost feel his presence next to her. She stepped behind the first of the cars and continued to slowly work her way toward the back.

"I'm more than that," he continued. "A vampire is nothing more than a mindless killing machine. Vampires weren't cultured gentleman like the movies portray. They were little more than zombies who ate blood instead of brains. They were truly non-discriminating. They made a mess too. I don't make a mess. I don't even leave a wound. Just a little prick, so small you could barely see it."

Faith stepped behind the second car, heart pounding. "Oh yeah," she said, "you're an artist."

"Oh, I'm no artist," he said, his voice nearly on top of her. "I'm an angel. *The* angel. Of death!"

He shrieked, and Faith caught movement out of the corner of her eye just as she stepped behind the third car. She whirled around, but the killer hit her before she could bring her weapon to bear. He knocked her to the ground, sending her gun skittering away underneath the car.

She rolled to her feet and came up just in time to see the killer's snarling face as he swung something toward her. She blocked his swing, catching his bicep with her palm. As she did, she saw the gleam of the needle in his hand. Her eyes widened, and she chopped at his wrist. He pulled back and swung again.

She leaned back, the needle slicing the air inches from her face. When the killer's arm passed her, she rushed forward, driving him back to the wall. She pinned his arm to his chest and gouged at his eyes, hoping to distract him long enough to wrestle the syringe from his grasp.

He growled and snapped at her fingers like an animal. She narrowly avoided having the tips of her fingers bitten off. Her recoil allowed him to regain his balance, and with a cry, he shoved her backwards to the ground.

She fell with a grunt and started to stand, but he leapt onto her and drove the needle downward toward her neck. She caught his wrist with both of hers, crossing them like an X and pushing upwards with all of her might.

The killer grinned and forced his weight down onto her, slowly driving the needle toward her neck. Faith tried to trap his ankle with her foot, but the killer either had experience with jiu-jitsu or just happened to know what she was trying, because he spread his legs over hers and pinned her.

"Time to go to sleep, FBI," he said, grinning maniacally at her.

She could smell the acrid stench of his breath as he leaned slowly closer. Images flashed in her mind of Trammell, grinning the same evil grin as he sliced her open, cutting her and laughing as he said, "Let's see how you bleed, little girl."

A burst of rage traveled through her. With a yell, she pushed him off of her. His eyes widened in surprise at her strength, and before he could recover, she kicked him hard. Her shoe impacted his nose, and she heard a satisfying crunch as the bone shattered.

He cried out and fell backward. She jumped on top of him and grabbed the arm holding the needle in both of hers. With a cry, she spun around and extended the arm across her chest, wrenching it at the elbow.

He screamed in pain, and she kept twisting his arm, but he held onto the needle with a death grip. He turned toward her, and above his shattered, bloody nose, she saw pure hate in his eyes. He yelled, and with sudden superhuman strength, he pulled his arm free. The needle slid along Faith's forearm as he did, and for a terrifying moment, Faith feared the needle had punctured her skin.

She took a moment to check herself, and that moment was her crucial mistake. Her arm showed no mark from the needle, but when she turned her attention back to the killer, he was already swinging the needle toward her neck.

Time slowed down. Faith had time to feel surprised at how calm she was. She expected to struggle against death, to rage against the dying of the light, as that one poem she had to write an analysis of in college had said. Instead, she found she was ready. She had fought a war. She had survived a serial killer. She had brought several other killers to justice. She suspected that one day she would meet the killer that would finally beat her. Her only regret was that she wouldn't get to catch the Donkey Killer's copycat after all.

Just before the needle reached her neck, she saw a flash of brown and black as Turk leapt in between her and the killer and clamped his jaws shut over his wrist.

Time snapped to full speed in an instant, and Faith stared in shock as the killer cried out in pain, falling to the ground while Turk shook his arm, his teeth slicing his wrist to ribbons. Somehow, the killer still managed to hold onto the needle. Faith rushed him, but he kicked out at her. His foot impacted her squarely in her solar plexus, and she fell to the ground, gasping for breath.

She rolled to her side and saw her gun. It lay a few yards away underneath the car.

She turned back to the fight to see the killer scrambling backwards, Turk still gripping his bloodied arm. He punched at Turk, landing hard blows to the dog's head and neck, but the big shepherd weathered the blows without releasing his arm.

Still struggling to regain her wind, Faith started crawling toward her weapon. She reached it just as Turk yelped in shock.

She grabbed the gun and turned to see the killer on top of Turk. He grabbed the needle from the hand Turk held and lifted it high.

Faith aimed and fired. The report of the gun was deafening in the confined space of the tunnel and Faith's hearing disappeared as her ears rang loudly. Turk, whose hearing was far more sensitive than Faith's, yelped again and released the killer, scrambling out from under him and shaking his head from side to side as he backed away.

The killer shrieked, and Faith decided it was a mercy she couldn't hear him. He clutched his arm to his chest. Where a hand had been a moment earlier was now a mangled, twisted mass of flesh. The needle and its deadly poison were nowhere to be seen.

Faith regained her feet and trained her weapon on the killer. "Stand down!" she commanded.

The killer looked at Faith, and Faith could see in his eyes that he knew it was over. She approached swiftly and pushed him onto his stomach, keeping her weapon trained on him until she planted her knee in between his shoulder blades.

She cuffed him, and as her hearing returned, she was disgusted to find he was crying softly. She yanked him to his feet and walked him toward the platform, Turk following.

"You have no idea how lucky you are that you didn't kill my dog," she snarled in his ear.

"Faith!" Michael's voice called, echoing through the tunnel.

She saw the beam of a flashlight shine through the tunnel, then another, then another.

"Over here!" she called.

Michael reached her just as she dragged the killer back onto the platform. Rameses and Wales were with him, along with ten other uniforms, all with weapons drawn.

She handed the killer—still weeping—to Rameses. "He had a poisoned needle," she said. "I haven't found it yet. Take Turk and look for the needle."

"I'll do that," Rameses said. "Damn good work, Special Agent."

"Are you hurt?" Michael asked, holstering his weapon and jogging over to her.

"Me?" she said. "No, not at all." She grinned tiredly and offered a thumbs up. "Right as rain."

Turk barked, and Faith looked over to see he had found the needle shattered, the deadly poison soaked into the dust and dirt of the platform. Rameses nodded at the dog, and he trotted happily over to where Faith and Michael stood.

Michael couldn't resist a chuckle as he ruffled Turk's fur. "Your mom's crazy, you know that?"

Turk barked in agreement, and Faith and Michael shared a laugh.

Faith looked over at the officers—who handled the killer with just slightly less roughness than would constitute a crime—and smiled softly. This might be the last collar she ever made, but she could claim to go out on a high note.

"I owe you a steak dinner," Michael told her.

"You owe me a lot of steak dinners," she countered.

"Well, we'll start with the one and go from there," he said. "I know a great steakhouse near the hotel."

"Can't wait," she said.

The three of them followed the officers and their despondent killer out of the platform and through the tunnel back to the terminal. *All in all, not a bad day's work,* Faith thought.

She looked down at Turk and grinned. "Guess I owe *you* a steak dinner, huh, buddy?"

Turk cast her a look that said Faith owed her a *lot* of steak dinners. She laughed and reached down to ruffle his fur. "Good dog."

CHAPTER TWENTY THREE

"Think he'll get the death penalty?" Michael asked.

Rameses shook his head. "DOJ might try to claim this is a Federal case because the first victim was a juror on the Hornfeldt case, but it's pretty clear that the case wasn't a motive for Gaston. The state might agree to let Gaston be tried in Federal court, but even if they do, he's clearly insane. I doubt he'll ever even stand trial."

Michael frowned. "Lovely. So, he gets to spend his days in a nice padded room."

"Between you and me," Rameses said, "I'd rather be in jail than a mental hospital. I've seen those places before working other cases. It's bad news."

Faith listened idly while Michael and Rameses discussed the fate of Charles Gaston, forty-one, the killer who would go down in history as the Subway Vampire. Gaston, alternating between fits of laughter and bouts of moodiness, had offered little in the way of coherent explanation for his crimes. One moment, he would rant about how horrible people were and how they deserved to die. The next, he would claim to be an agent of God sent to Earth to rid the world of rudeness.

At the moment, the three of them watched as a negotiator attempted to calm Gaston and elicit some form of intelligible answer from him. Gaston was in the middle of one of his manic episodes, laughing and jerking at the chains that bound his hands to the table.

"Are we sure this isn't an act?" Michael asked. "He managed to remain calm and collected when he was at the terminal. Now suddenly he's batshit insane?"

"Happens all the time," Rameses said. "I'm not a psychologist, but I've seen plenty of killers lose their shit after they're caught. Sometimes it's an act, and they're playing a part, hoping that no one will figure them out before they can get a not-guilty play. A lot of times, it's real. People like him—" he lifted his chin toward Gaston "—create this fantasy world where everything plays by whatever twisted rules they've made in their heads. When that world collapses around them, they have nothing left to tether them to reality."

"So, is Gaston the former or the latter?"

"The latter, definitely," Rameses said. "You can tell by his eyes. They never seem to focus on anything."

They focused well enough when he killed people and staged their bodies, Faith thought to herself.

She didn't say it out loud. She believed Gaston really was insane. She didn't believe that excused him from his actions. There was a distance between believing that people were demons out to kill you and believing that the proper response for someone brushing past you at work was to poison them and leave their bodies so you could watch people pass them without knowing they were dead.

"What's next for you two?" Rameses asked.

"Oh, you know," Michael said, "back home and back to the drawing board. First, I owe my partner here a good steak dinner for once more being right."

"You taking her to Nellie's?" Rameses asked.

"You know it," Michael replied with a grin.

Rameses laughed. "So, is this meal for her or for you?"

"Does it matter?" Michael asked.

The two men shared another laugh as the negotiator left the interrogation room, shaking her head. "This one's done," she said, twisting her finger in a circle next to her temple. "Completely gone. In my professional opinion."

"Yeah, I thought as much," Rameses said. "Well, we'll keep him in the Special cell for now until they pack him up and ship him to the cuckoo's nest. At least there he won't be able to poison anyone."

"I don't know," the negotiator said. "Did you ever see that movie about that inmate who impersonated a doctor at a mental hospital and went on a killing spree?"

"Yeah, but that guy wasn't a patient. He actually thought he was a doctor until he went back and started remembering who he really was."

Rameses and the negotiator left the room, continuing to trade stories. Faith and Michael watched them go, then turned to each other.

"Well," Michael said, "I guess I owe you a dinner."

Faith smiled. "You owe me a lot of dinners."

***

Faith had to hand it to Michael. The man knew a properly cooked steak. The filet Faith ordered was soft and smooth as butter and cooked to a perfect rare temperature.

"You know how hard it is to find a restaurant that actually knows how to cook a rare steak?" Faith said in between bites.

"It's an endangered species," Michael agreed, sawing contentedly at his ribeye. "I'm a medium-rare man myself, but if you don't know what rare is, you don't know what medium-rare is either."

"True that," Faith agreed, eating another bite.

Next to them, Turk happily wolfed down his own steak, this one also rare at Faith's insistence. They sat what felt like a football field away from the other guests at a small table near the busboy's station. The restaurant owner reluctantly allowed the two agents to eat there with Turk considering their service to the city in catching Gaston, but he made sure they ate as far away from the other customers as possible. From the brief glimpses Faith had gotten of the other guests, she felt that Turk had much better table manners than most of the other guests had.

Not that it mattered. It wasn't like they were going to be regulars here. Besides, the food *was* good, and good food excused a lot of rudeness.

"You think if Gaston had eaten like this, he might have forgiven those people who ignored him?" Michael asked, echoing Faith's thought.

"Maybe," Faith said. "They say the way to a man's heart is through his stomach."

"Boy, ain't that the truth," Michael said. "Ellie makes the best damn pork ribs you've ever had. I swear, if I ever go off the rails and land myself in trouble, my last meal will be her pork spareribs slathered in thick, honey bourbon barbecue sauce." He patted his belly. "Five years from now when you look at me and wonder how on Earth I let myself go so badly, the answer is those ribs."

Faith offered a smile, but Michael saw right through it. He sighed and said, "Faith, I know you don't want to talk about this, but we really do need to talk about Ellie."

Faith sighed herself and set her fork onto her plate. She met Michael's eyes and said, "Why, Michael? Why does it matter? Why can't we just be friends and not be involved in each other's personal lives?"

"Because I can't be friends with someone who isn't honest with me," he said, "not even if that person is my partner."

"There's a difference between being honest and being completely open," Faith said. "I'm not lying to you. I just don't feel a need to share every thought that pops into my head. I know that you like to share everything with your friends, but I don't, Michael. I'm a very private person. You know this."

"Yes, but this isn't about you," Michael said. "It's about me and Ellie, and I'd very much like to know why you don't like her."

Faith sighed again. She looked away and sighed a third time. Finally, she said, "Michael, this is only going to upset you. Things are already … well, things are tense enough between us right now. I really don't want to make things worse by opening this can of worms."

"The fact that there's a can of worms to open already makes things tense," Michael said. "Hiding the worms will only prevent us from working on easing that tension. This is the first step toward fixing things," he said. "The first step toward getting to the point where we can be comfortable around each other."

Faith didn't reply right away. She knew Michael well enough to know that what she had to say would do little to make him feel comfortable around her.

She also knew him well enough to know that he wouldn't budge from this. Not telling him would only guarantee the eventual—and probably not too eventual—end of their friendship.

So, she sighed and said, "All right, Michael. If you want to know why, then here goes. I don't like Ellie because I don't trust her."

Michael stared at her in shock. He blinked and said, "You … you don't trust her? Why?"

Michael's shock seemed genuine, but behind the shock, Faith thought she could detect the slightest hint of guilt. Deep down, he didn't trust her either. Faith had suspected that, and now that she knew it was true, she knew for sure that this conversation would drive a wedge deeply between them.

She sighed. "Well, after Turk reacted the way that he did, I—"

Michael's eyes hardened immediately. "Turk," he said. "So, your *dog* doesn't like her, and you assume that means she's bad news."

"Turk's almost never wrong, Michael," Faith said.

"Emphasis on *almost*, Faith. If you'll recall, he was wrong twice in the past week."

"I recall," Faith said, a little brittlely, "but he's right more often than he's wrong."

"Yeah, and so am I," he countered, "and I don't think she's bad news."

"It's not just Turk, Michael," Faith said. "The whole situation is suspicious. She's been separated from her husband for months now, years, I think, right?"

"Faith, it's not so simple as tearing her wedding ring off and saying, 'I'm not married anymore, nyah nyah nyah.' She has a lot of finances bound up in her marriage."

"And what's she done to correct that issue?" Faith asked. "Has she made any progress at all, or has she just waited for it to magically happen?"

"Faith, not everyone is ..." Michael sighed and looked down at his plate for a moment. When he lifted his head, the corners of his lips were turned down. "Not everyone is as strong as you. Not everyone can get cut literally to pieces and recover from that."

Faith's knee twitched and a stab of guilt joined the stab of pain. "I'm not as strong as you think I am, Michael," she said.

"Oh, enough with the sympathetic self-abasement," Michael said, believing her statement to be for his benefit and not the actual truth. "You can get literally stabbed and punched and beaten and shake it off. That's what made you a great Marine. It's what makes you a great agent. Unfortunately, it also makes you very cold and distant and emotionally unavailable."

Faith weathered the jab, knowing that Michael's frustration was prompting him to lash out. "We're not talking about you and me, Michael," she said calmly. "We agreed that we weren't right for each other, and we still feel that way. This isn't some misguided jealous response, Michael. This is about Ellie. Ellie is lying to you, Michael."

"That's your opinion," he said icily.

"It is," she agreed, "but it's not an opinion I've arrived at idly. When we were at dinner, I saw the way she acted around you."

"The way she acted around me?" he said. "What are you talking about?"

Faith took a breath. "When you kissed her, she would tense up. Just slightly, just enough that you wouldn't notice unless you were looking for it, but—"

"Were you looking for it?" Michael challenged.

"No," she said. "No, I was—"

"Then how could you tell?" he said.

Faith sighed. "Can we just drop it, Michael? This is why I didn't want to talk about this in the first place."

"No, come on," Michael said, "I want you to tell me how. How could you tell that she was tense when I kissed her?"

Faith shook her head and resigned herself to the conversation. "Her shoulders would stiffen, her cheeks would freeze briefly, and her hands would start to cross over her chest before she would catch herself and stop."

"Really?" Michael said.

He no doubt intended the question to come out sarcastically, but all Faith could sense was hurt.

"Really," she said softly, "and whenever the conversation turned to the future between you guys, she would always change the subject. She was surprisingly good at that. I don't think she committed to a single plan you made."

"Well, I wasn't planning," he argued, "I was just daydreaming. You know how it is when you're in the first flush of romance."

"Yes," Faith said, "I do. I very much do. That's how I know that Ellie doesn't see a future with you. When you're in the first blush of romance, you daydream *with* your partner. You go along with all of their foolish plans and you dream of forever even if you know it's silly. When he mentions going to Europe or the Caribbean or on a cruise, you talk about how much fun you'll have and what you'll wear and what the food will be like, and you allow yourself to imagine it's real. You don't laugh and then change the subject. You don't say things like 'Well, we'll see,' or 'I don't know, maybe.'"

"*You* don't say those things," Michael said, "but *you* haven't lost your husband of ten years to another woman and then been forced to keep his last name for years because you haven't been allowed to be your own person ever since you took that name for yours."

"Michael, it's clear that you aren't going to believe me," Faith said, "and that's fine. For what it's worth, I hope I'm wrong. For what it's worth, it also doesn't matter what I think. If you like her, then that's all that matters. You'll be all right whether this works out or not, so just enjoy it while you have it, and if things work out, then wonderful."

"Well, listen, though," he said plaintively. "Listen to me and let me explain to you why I think you're wrong. I think you owe me that much."

Faith sighed and lifted her hand, letting it fall back onto her lap. "All right," she said tonelessly.

"Faith, she is so kind to me. She's so sweet, you wouldn't believe it. She always cooks for me. I mean breakfast every morning when I wake up and dinner on the table when I come home. She gives me the best massages every day. That's not the same as sex, okay? There's nothing in it for her. She just does it to make me feel good."

"That's wonderful, Michael," Faith said. "I'm glad."

"No, listen," Michael said, his tone almost desperate. "When I talk to her, she doesn't feel a need to judge me the way so many other people in my life do. She doesn't have to follow it up with some sarcastic jab or some advice that's really just a thin way to disguise disapproval."

Faith's lips thinned a little when she heard that. She didn't know for sure that Michael meant that as a jab to her, but his biggest complaint when they dated was that she was overly judgmental.

Actually, that was his second biggest complaint. His biggest was that she was cold.

"And she's so …" he sighed. "She's …"

"Warm?" Faith offered.

"Yes," he said. "She's warm and sweet and soft and caring, and coming home to her is like coming home to a break from all the shit I have to deal with on a daily fucking basis with this damned job. Pardon my French, but you know how it is. This job will wear you down and wear you down and wear you down and wear you down until there's nothing left. You …" he waved his hand at her, "… you're like a brick wall. You can stand there and laugh while you get hit over and over and over, and you'll just lift your hands and ask for more."

Another twinge of pain ran through Faith's knees. She lowered her eyes while Michael continued. "I can't, Faith," he said softly. "I can't handle it. Not by myself. Not without someone to come home to to help me forget about all of this."

Faith understood now why Michael needed her approval so badly. He suspected Ellie of being dishonest with him, too, but he needed to believe that she really was as wonderful as he needed her to be. He needed to have that soft place to come home to, that calm, kind person who could take his pain away and give him a reason to believe that everything would be okay.

He had sought that from Faith, and in Faith, he had found a strong, unyielding woman who shared herself only reluctantly and offered comfort in the form of cold logic and a Marine veteran's refusal to listen to excuses. In Ellie, he found the gentleness and kindness and purity that he could find nowhere else in his life.

He needed her, but as much as he needed her, he knew she wasn't what he needed her to be, and he needed Faith to ease his doubts so he could pretend, at least for a little while, that he'd found his happily ever after.

She couldn't.

"Michael," she said, "I hope you enjoy every moment with Ellie."

Michael smiled softly, but his smile disappeared when Faith said reluctantly, "But be ready for it to end."

He sat silently for a long moment. Faith met his eyes, her heart breaking with every passing second. After a moment, he said, "Well, thank you for talking to me. I appreciate your honesty."

They finished the rest of their meal in silence. That silence remained unbroken as they drove home to Philadelphia. Faith dropped Michael off at his house. Through the window, she could see Ellie lift a bottle to her lips and head to the front door to greet him.

She looked at Michael, and by the grim expression on his face, she could tell he saw her too.

"Are we still friends, Michael?" she asked softly.

"Yeah," he said, his voice light and airy. "Yeah, of course."

He offered a smile which didn't reach his eyes and bothered to keep it only for a second before getting out of the car and walking up the steps to the front door.

Faith watched as Ellie opened the door and pulled Michael into her arms. She held him close for a long moment, then pulled away just enough to press her lips to his and kiss him deeply.

From the backseat, Turk growled low in his throat. Faith reached behind and scratched his neck. "It's okay, boy," she said.

She backed out of the driveway and started for home. The moon was full and bright and cast a soft glow over the city, which, like the city she just left, never truly slept. She glanced at the moon and said, "No stars tonight."

Turk whined softly, and Faith reached behind again to stroke his fur.

CHAPTER TWENTY FOUR

"David?"

David looked up from his capellini. "Yes?"

Faith pushed at a piece of gnocchi with her fork and said, "Do you think I'm cold?"

He frowned and reached forward, laying his hand on her forehead. "You feel all right to me, but you can have my jacket if you want."

Faith chuckled and said, "You're sweet, David, but that's not what I meant."

"What did you mean?" he asked. "Cold like a cold, unfeeling bitch?"

She laughed again and said, "Well, I didn't mean that extreme, but yeah, I guess so."

"Well, no," he said. "I don't think you're cold at all. I think you're tough and no-nonsense. I think you don't take crap from anybody. I think you're strong-willed, and I think you can sometimes be a little too blunt, but I think you care fiercely for those close to you, more than anyone I've ever met."

She smiled at him and decided she was falling in love with him. "Thank you," she said. "That's actually really nice to hear right now."

"Why?" he asked.

"Why is it nice to hear?"

"No, I mean why did you ask me if you were cold? Did someone say you were cold?"

"Not recently," Faith said, "but it's been mentioned before."

"What prompted you to think about that all of a sudden?"

She sighed. "Nothing. I'm sorry. I just … felt a little insecure, I guess."

He took her hand in his and said, "Faith? What's going on?"

She sighed and said, "You have to promise not to tell anyone."

"Oh, I can't promise that," he said seriously. "I have like, a dozen friends who hang on every word you tell me. If I don't pass along the goods the moment I hear it, I'll lose them."

Faith rolled her eyes. "Well, if you're not gonna take this seriously."

He laughed and said, "I won't tell anyone, Faith."

She took a deep breath and said, "Michael's been dating this girl, Ellie."

"The divorcee?"

"Not yet, and in my opinion, not ever unless he's the one who pulls the trigger."

"You think she's still in love with him?"

Faith thought a moment. "No," she said, "I don't think so. But she's not in love with Michael."

"Wow," he said. "What makes you say that?"

Faith told him about the visit to Michael's house. She glossed over most of the details but related the way she stiffened at his touch and the way she would avoid the subject of their future.

"Hmm," he said when she finished. "Well, I won't lie. That sounds pretty bad."

"It does, right?" she said. "I just …"

Her voice trailed off. David waited patiently until she worked up the courage to say what she had to say next.

"I wonder if maybe I'm imagining it," she said. "Not that she's being weird, but that the reason may not be what I think it is. Or maybe I am imagining that she doesn't like him, and I'm just jealous because she's taking Michael away from me. Not that I want Michael back, but … I mean—"

"You miss your friend."

"Yes," she said, "I do. I want to go back to the way we were. We had this whole buddy cop thing going on, and it actually made working fun. Now, things are just so tense and draining, and I spend the whole time moody and irritable and just desperate to come home. I just feel like ever since he started dating her that he's been pulling away from me, and I know he wants me to like her, but I just can't unsee what I saw, and—"

"Faith," David said calmly, "it's okay."

"It's not though, David," she said, "I feel …"

"Faith, you won't be able to make everyone happy. Sometimes, you'll do and say things that hurt people. Sometimes, it'll even be your fault. This time, though, I don't think it is. You tried not to talk about it, but he forced you to. You could have lied to him, but you know he would have seen through it. So, you were honest."

"What do I do, though?" she asked. "How do I fix this?"

"You don't," he said gently. "You just let this run its course. Either things will work out between Michael and Ellie, in which case you'll apologize, and he'll lord it over you for a few months—" Faith chuckled, "—or things won't work out between them, in which case he'll ignore you for a few months because he feels ashamed, then dejectedly shuffle up and mutter an apology which you'll lord over him for the rest of his life."

"Watch it, buster," she said, smiling at him.

"Buster?" he said. "Buster?"

Faith reddened, "Would you like me make up a worse nickname?"

"Buster?" he said, laughing. "Oh Faith, please. Please call me Buster for the rest of my life."

"Shut up!" she said, slapping him playfully.

He laughed and continued to tease her about the name, and by the time they reached home, she had forgotten all about Ellie.

***

"I'm sorry to hear about your meeting with SAC Monroe," Doctor West said. "I truly hope this won't have serious consequences to your career."

Faith chuckled. "You know it's going to have serious consequences to my career."

"Yes," he said, nodding slowly. "Yes, I apologize for offering that foolish attempt at comfort. Even psychologists are human, I'm afraid."

"No need to apologize," Faith said. "I got myself into this mess."

"Should this result in … well, should the worst happen, I want to assure you, I'll still be available to treat you."

Faith smiled. "Thank you, Doctor West, but I don't think they'll fire me. I've become somewhat of a celebrity in the Bureau over the past couple of years."

"Solving four high-profile cases back-to-back will do that," he said with a smile.

Faith nodded modestly. "Anyway, I don't think they'll fire me. It's bad publicity to fire your star agent. What they'll do is promote me to a cool sounding but unimportant desk job that will look to the outside world like an expansion of responsibility but will really just be keeping me out of the way. Then they'll leave me there to die or reach retirement age and take my pension."

"Would it be completely crass of me to say that doesn't sound like a bad option?" Doctor West offered with a slight smile.

"Terribly crass," Faith said, "but … there are days where I think that you might be right."

"How do you feel today?" he asked.

She paused a moment. "I … cannot work a desk job."

"No," he agreed, "you can't."

"I wish I could, though."

"Do you wish you could?" he asked. "Or do you wish the job you have now was easier?"

"I wish I could work the copycat killer case," she blurted out. "I wish I could have that case so I could get this damned monkey off my back. Yes, I know my motivation is wrong. Yes, I know it's bad that I'm fixated on Trammell, and I know you're going to tell me that it's unhealthy of me to project my feelings of fear and helplessness onto the copycat killer, but I can't stop. I won't stop."

"Those are too different things, Faith," Doctor West said. "To say you can't stop is to say you lack the ability to cease a certain activity. To say you won't stop is to say you're unwilling to cease a certain activity."

Faith rolled her eyes. "Okay, grammar police. I *won't* stop."

"Words have power, Faith," Doctor West said, refusing to be deflected. "Don't say you can't do something when what you mean is you won't do something. When you say you can't do something when you won't do something, you excuse your *choice* by claiming a lack of ability to choose. In doing so, you not only reinforce poor decision-making, but you also demean your sense of agency."

Faith blinked in surprise. "Wow," she said. "That was a lot of really smart sounding words."

"Every one of which you understood," he said. "I won't tell you that it's not a good idea for you to pursue the copycat case. I won't tell you it's a bad idea either. I won't do either because it won't matter what I tell you. You've already made your choice. The only thing I'll tell you to do is to take ownership of that choice and every consequence that comes from it."

"I will," she said. "I already told you that I know I got myself into this mess."

"Your professional consequences will pale in comparison to your personal consequences, Faith, some of which you're already experiencing."

"Already experiencing? What are you talking about? Wait, are you saying that Michael and I are fighting because of the copycat killer case?"

"I didn't say that," Doctor West responded. "You did."

Faith felt a flash of irritation. "Don't play word games with me. Is that what you're saying?"

"What I said was that you're already suffering personal consequences due to your obsession with the copycat killer. What you said was that you and Michael were fighting because of your obsession with the case. You must believe that your relationship with Michael has been impacted by your obsession with the copycat killer case."

She opened her mouth to protest but closed it without saying anything. Deep down, a part of her did believe that. In fact, now that she thought about it, Michael had pointed out that since he told her about the copycat killer, she had been moody and distant and cold. The fights over Ellie had come after.

She looked away and crossed her arms in front of her.

"That's a—"

"Yes, I know it's a defensive posture, thank you."

"Faith, I say none of this to hurt you," he said gently.

"I need this!" she said, hating how plaintive she sounded.

"Do you?" he asked gently.

"I …" her lower lip trembled. "I … I *hate* that he had me like that. I can handle being in pain. I can handle being hurt. I can handle dying, but I cannot handle being so … utterly powerless. He tied me to a chair, told me he was going to make me scream, then did it. I promised myself I wouldn't give him the satisfaction of screaming, and I screamed. I screamed and cried, and I couldn't stop myself. I couldn't …" her voice trailed off, and she once more looked away from Doctor West.

"Faith, you were tortured," Doctor West said softly. "You can't seriously expect yourself to refrain from a natural physical reaction to extreme pain. That's not a sign of mental deficiency, Faith. Frankly, to *not* scream and cry would be a sign of mental deficiency."

"It doesn't matter," she said. "It doesn't matter because I was utterly powerless, and I've been utterly powerless ever since that day. It doesn't matter until I beat him, and I know it's not really him, and a small part of me will always carry the memory of that chair, but if I can beat him, if I can beat *this* Donkey Killer, then that part of me will be much smaller."

"You haven't *been* powerless," he countered. "You've *felt* powerless."

"No," Faith said. "I know words have power, and these words are the honest truth. I have *been* powerless since Trammell cut me because I cannot stop seeing and hearing and feeling and *smelling* him since that day, and I have lashed out and pushed away those closest to me, and I will lose the only people in my life that I care about if I don't stop him."

Her words hung heavy in the air for a long while. Doctor West looked down at his chin for a long moment before finally saying, "I'll offer you this thought before we close our session for today, Faith. If you beat this copycat killer, the part of you that's tied to Trammell's chair will become much smaller, maybe even small enough to manage for the rest of your life. If, on the other hand, you choose to stand up out of the chair yourself and walk away from it, then that part of you will disappear."

His words now hung in the air, silently and just as heavy. After a moment, he again broke the silence by saying, "I know you'll do whatever you want regardless of what I or anyone else says, but please consider my advice. You *can* overcome your trauma. You just have to be willing to sacrifice your fear."

Faith considered his words as she drove home. She knew he was right. If it were someone else in her position, she would very bluntly—very "coldly"—tell them to move on.

It was so much easier said than done, though.

EPILOGUE

"I'll be honest with you, Bold. The only reason you still work at this Bureau is because you're a media darling right now."

Faith sat in the upholstered chair in front of the Boss's desk. The Boss stood in front of the desk, staring down at her with a deep scowl. His tone was uncharacteristically subdued, which made it all the more sobering. To his right, Special Agent Clark stood with his fingers interlaced in front of him, his face a mix of frustration at Faith and a desire to be anywhere other than present for the dressing-down of a fellow Special Agent. Turk sat next to Faith, staring at Clark with a strange look on his face. Outside, Michael glowered through the window, having been repeatedly told to leave the office until finally Faith told him it was okay and that he should leave.

"I'm sorry you feel that way, sir," she said calmly.

"I would absolutely love to hear why you think I should feel differently," he said in that quietly menacing tone.

"Because, sir, in the past twenty months, I've put four major serial killers behind bars. In three of those cases, I've intervened and saved the lives of would-be victims, and in all four of those cases, I've apprehended those criminals at great personal risk including loss of my own life. You asked me when I returned if I was ready to come back to work, and I have proven time and again that I am. I acknowledge that I violated policy when I intervened—"

"Interfered," the Boss interrupted.

"—in the Copycat Killer case, but I don't believe that justifies removing me from the field."

"In short, the good outweighs the bad."

"That's an incomplete way of putting it, sir."

"It's a succinct way of putting it," he replied, "unfettered by bullshit self-flattery. Bold, I shouldn't have to explain to an agent with nearly ten years of experience that interfering in a case you have been specifically told to stay away from is a major breach of conduct. I shouldn't have to explain to you that my decision to deny you the copycat killer case was out of concern that your mental state was not such that you could handle the case, and I shouldn't have to explain to someone of your intelligence that your behavior thus far has absolutely justified my decision."

Faith's jaw tightened, but the Boss had left her no room to retort, so she remained silent.

"I am sorry for what happened to you," the Boss said, his tone surprisingly gentle and sincere. "I am. But I have a job to do, and so do you. Fortunately for you, you are as talented of an agent as you flatter yourself to be, and it doesn't go unnoticed that you've brought to justice several killers who would certainly have killed many more had you not been there to stop them. So, despite your flagrant disobedience, I will allow you to remain in the field."

"Thank you, sir," Faith said, relaxing, "you won't regret it."

"But," the Boss said, "you will report to Special Agent Clark."

Clark's head snapped up in alarm. Faith stared at the Boss in shock.

"You heard me," the Boss said. "You will report to Clark a minimum of once per day with a summary of your day's activities. At any time he sees fit, he can call or visit you to ensure you're being honest with your account. If he issues you an order, you will follow it as though it came from me. Actually, you will follow it much better than the way you follow my orders."

"Sir, please," Faith said. "I can't work with a babysitter."

"Tough shit, Bold," he said. "I can't trust you to keep your nose clean, so Clark will wipe it for you until I'm convinced you can do it yourself. You're on probation, Bold. It's this or a desk."

Faith took a deep breath, closed her eyes, and said through gritted teeth, "I'll report to Clark, sir."

"Good," the Boss said. "And if I so much as catch you reading a news article about the copycat killer, I will personally take your badge and gun from you, do you understand me?"

"Yes, sir."

"Outstanding. Get the hell out of my office."

Faith stood to leave. Clark followed Faith and Turk out of the office, and when they were out of the Boss's line of sight, Clark stepped closer and said, "Faith, listen, I—"

Turk lunged at Clark suddenly, barking and snapping at him. Clark leaped back, alarmed as Faith threw herself on top of Turk and said, "Turk! Stop it!"

The other agents in the office looked at them, and Faith saw the knob of the Boss's office door turn. She stood up quickly and when the Boss stepped outside to see what the commotion was, Clark said, "It's fine, everything's fine. I accidentally stepped on Turk's tail, and he yelped. No big deal."

The others returned to work, and the Boss went back into his office. Clark glanced at Turk, then at Faith, then left for his desk.

Faith watched him walk away for a moment, then left the office, pulling Turk with her. She tried to tell herself that there was nothing to read into in Turk's behavior. After all, he had made mistakes.

He rarely made mistakes.

What was it that Turk thought he sensed about Clark?

NOW AVAILABLE!

SO FAR GONE
(A Faith Bold Mystery—Book 5)

When the coroner can't decipher the mysterious plaster residue on each of a new killer's victims, FBI Special Agent Faith Bold know she is up against a diabolical and mastermind killer—and that she will need her K9 German Shepherd, Turk, to help crack the case. But Faith, still reeling from her own demons, is fragile, and even with Turk's strength and loyalty, Faith knows that this just may be the case that pushes her over the edge.

"A masterpiece of thriller and mystery."
—Books and Movie Reviews, Roberto Mattos (re Once Gone)

SO FAR GONE is Book #5 in a long-anticipated new series by #1 bestseller and USA Today bestselling author Blake Pierce, whose bestseller Once Gone (a free download) has received over 7,000 five star ratings and reviews.

FBI Special Agent Faith Bold doesn't believe she can ever return to the force after the trauma she's been through. Suffering from past demons, she feels unfit for duty and content to retire—until Turk walks into her life.

Turk, a former Marine Corps dog, wounded in battle, suffers from his own demons. But he never lets it show as he gives everything to Faith to get her back on her feet.

Each are slow to warm up to each other, but when they do, they are inseparable. Each is equally determined to hunt down the demons chasing them, whatever the cost, and to watch each other's backs—even at the risk of their own life.

A page-turning and harrowing crime thriller featuring a brilliant and tortured FBI agent, the Faith Bold series is a riveting mystery, packed with non-stop action, suspense, twists and turns, revelations, and driven by a breakneck pace that will keep you flipping pages late into the night. Fans of Rachel Caine, Teresa Driscoll and Robert Dugoni are sure to fall in love.

Future books in the series are now also available.

"An edge of your seat thriller in a new series that keeps you turning pages! ...So many twists, turns and red herrings… I can't wait to see what happens next."
—Reader review (Her Last Wish)

"A strong, complex story about two FBI agents trying to stop a serial killer. If you want an author to capture your attention and have you guessing, yet trying to put the pieces together, Pierce is your author!"
—Reader review (Her Last Wish)

"A typical Blake Pierce twisting, turning, roller coaster ride suspense thriller. Will have you turning the pages to the last sentence of the last chapter!!!"
—Reader review (City of Prey)

"Right from the start we have an unusual protagonist that I haven't seen done in this genre before. The action is nonstop… A very atmospheric novel that will keep you turning pages well into the wee hours."
—Reader review (City of Prey)

"Everything that I look for in a book… a great plot, interesting characters, and grabs your interest right away. The book moves along at a breakneck pace and stays that way until the end. Now on go I to book two!"
—Reader review (Girl, Alone)

"Exciting, heart pounding, edge of your seat book… a must read for mystery and suspense readers!"
—Reader review (Girl, Alone)

Blake Pierce

Blake Pierce is the USA Today bestselling author of the RILEY PAGE mystery series, which includes seventeen books. Blake Pierce is also the author of the MACKENZIE WHITE mystery series, comprising fourteen books; of the AVERY BLACK mystery series, comprising six books; of the KERI LOCKE mystery series, comprising five books; of the MAKING OF RILEY PAIGE mystery series, comprising six books; of the KATE WISE mystery series, comprising seven books; of the CHLOE FINE psychological suspense mystery, comprising six books; of the JESSIE HUNT psychological suspense thriller series, comprising twenty-eight books; of the AU PAIR psychological suspense thriller series, comprising three books; of the ZOE PRIME mystery series, comprising six books; of the ADELE SHARP mystery series, comprising sixteen books, of the EUROPEAN VOYAGE cozy mystery series, comprising six books; of the LAURA FROST FBI suspense thriller, comprising eleven books; of the ELLA DARK FBI suspense thriller, comprising fourteen books (and counting); of the A YEAR IN EUROPE cozy mystery series, comprising nine books, of the AVA GOLD mystery series, comprising six books; of the RACHEL GIFT mystery series, comprising ten books (and counting); of the VALERIE LAW mystery series, comprising nine books (and counting); of the PAIGE KING mystery series, comprising eight books (and counting); of the MAY MOORE mystery series, comprising eleven books; of the CORA SHIELDS mystery series, comprising eight books (and counting); of the NICKY LYONS mystery series, comprising eight books (and counting), of the CAMI LARK mystery series, comprising eight books (and counting), of the AMBER YOUNG mystery series, comprising five books (and counting), of the DAISY FORTUNE mystery series, comprising five books (and counting), of the FIONA RED mystery series, comprising eight books (and counting), of the FAITH BOLD mystery series, comprising eight books (and counting), of the JULIETTE HART mystery series, comprising five books (and counting), of the MORGAN CROSS mystery series, comprising five books (and counting), and of the new FINN WRIGHT mystery series, comprising five books (and counting).

An avid reader and lifelong fan of the mystery and thriller genres, Blake loves to hear from you, so please feel free to visit www.blakepierceauthor.com to learn more and stay in touch.

BOOKS BY BLAKE PIERCE

FINN WRIGHT MYSTERY SERIES
WHEN YOU'RE MINE (Book #1)
WHEN YOU'RE SAFE (Book #2)
WHEN YOU'RE CLOSE (Book #3)
WHEN YOU'RE SLEEPING (Book #4)
WHEN YOU'RE SANE (Book #5)

MORGAN CROSS MYSTERY SERIES
FOR YOU (Book #1)
FOR RAGE (Book #2)
FOR LUST (Book #3)
FOR WRATH (Book #4)
FOREVER (Book #5)

JULIETTE HART MYSTERY SERIES
NOTHING TO FEAR (Book #1)
NOTHING THERE (Book #2)
NOTHING WATCHING (Book #3)
NOTHING HIDING (Book #4)
NOTHING LEFT (Book #5)

FAITH BOLD MYSTERY SERIES
SO LONG (Book #1)
SO COLD (Book #2)
SO SCARED (Book #3)
SO NORMAL (Book #4)
SO FAR GONE (Book #5)
SO LOST (Book #6)
SO ALONE (Book #7)
SO FORGOTTEN (Book #8)

FIONA RED MYSTERY SERIES
LET HER GO (Book #1)
LET HER BE (Book #2)
LET HER HOPE (Book #3)
LET HER WISH (Book #4)

LET HER LIVE (Book #5)
LET HER RUN (Book #6)
LET HER HIDE (Book #7)
LET HER BELIEVE (Book #8)

DAISY FORTUNE MYSTERY SERIES
NEED YOU (Book #1)
CLAIM YOU (Book #2)
CRAVE YOU (Book #3)
CHOOSE YOU (Book #4)
CHASE YOU (Book #5)

AMBER YOUNG MYSTERY SERIES
ABSENT PITY (Book #1)
ABSENT REMORSE (Book #2)
ABSENT FEELING (Book #3)
ABSENT MERCY (Book #4)
ABSENT REASON (Book #5)

CAMI LARK MYSTERY SERIES
JUST ME (Book #1)
JUST OUTSIDE (Book #2)
JUST RIGHT (Book #3)
JUST FORGET (Book #4)
JUST ONCE (Book #5)
JUST HIDE (Book #6)
JUST NOW (Book #7)
JUST HOPE (Book #8)

NICKY LYONS MYSTERY SERIES
ALL MINE (Book #1)
ALL HIS (Book #2)
ALL HE SEES (Book #3)
ALL ALONE (Book #4)
ALL FOR ONE (Book #5)
ALL HE TAKES (Book #6)
ALL FOR ME (Book #7)
ALL IN (Book #8)

CORA SHIELDS MYSTERY SERIES
UNDONE (Book #1)

UNWANTED (Book #2)
UNHINGED (Book #3)
UNSAID (Book #4)
UNGLUED (Book #5)
UNSTABLE (Book #6)
UNKNOWN (Book #7)
UNAWARE (Book #8)

MAY MOORE SUSPENSE THRILLER
NEVER RUN (Book #1)
NEVER TELL (Book #2)
NEVER LIVE (Book #3)
NEVER HIDE (Book #4)
NEVER FORGIVE (Book #5)
NEVER AGAIN (Book #6)
NEVER LOOK BACK (Book #7)
NEVER FORGET (Book #8)
NEVER LET GO (Book #9)
NEVER PRETEND (Book #10)
NEVER HESITATE (Book #11)

PAIGE KING MYSTERY SERIES
THE GIRL HE PINED (Book #1)
THE GIRL HE CHOSE (Book #2)
THE GIRL HE TOOK (Book #3)
THE GIRL HE WISHED (Book #4)
THE GIRL HE CROWNED (Book #5)
THE GIRL HE WATCHED (Book #6)
THE GIRL HE WANTED (Book #7)
THE GIRL HE CLAIMED (Book #8)

VALERIE LAW MYSTERY SERIES
NO MERCY (Book #1)
NO PITY (Book #2)
NO FEAR (Book #3)
NO SLEEP (Book #4)
NO QUARTER (Book #5)
NO CHANCE (Book #6)
NO REFUGE (Book #7)
NO GRACE (Book #8)
NO ESCAPE (Book #9)

RACHEL GIFT MYSTERY SERIES
HER LAST WISH (Book #1)
HER LAST CHANCE (Book #2)
HER LAST HOPE (Book #3)
HER LAST FEAR (Book #4)
HER LAST CHOICE (Book #5)
HER LAST BREATH (Book #6)
HER LAST MISTAKE (Book #7)
HER LAST DESIRE (Book #8)
HER LAST REGRET (Book #9)
HER LAST HOUR (Book #10)

AVA GOLD MYSTERY SERIES
CITY OF PREY (Book #1)
CITY OF FEAR (Book #2)
CITY OF BONES (Book #3)
CITY OF GHOSTS (Book #4)
CITY OF DEATH (Book #5)
CITY OF VICE (Book #6)

A YEAR IN EUROPE
A MURDER IN PARIS (Book #1)
DEATH IN FLORENCE (Book #2)
VENGEANCE IN VIENNA (Book #3)
A FATALITY IN SPAIN (Book #4)

ELLA DARK FBI SUSPENSE THRILLER
GIRL, ALONE (Book #1)
GIRL, TAKEN (Book #2)
GIRL, HUNTED (Book #3)
GIRL, SILENCED (Book #4)
GIRL, VANISHED (Book 5)
GIRL ERASED (Book #6)
GIRL, FORSAKEN (Book #7)
GIRL, TRAPPED (Book #8)
GIRL, EXPENDABLE (Book #9)
GIRL, ESCAPED (Book #10)
GIRL, HIS (Book #11)
GIRL, LURED (Book #12)
GIRL, MISSING (Book #13)

GIRL, UNKNOWN (Book #14)

LAURA FROST FBI SUSPENSE THRILLER

ALREADY GONE (Book #1)
ALREADY SEEN (Book #2)
ALREADY TRAPPED (Book #3)
ALREADY MISSING (Book #4)
ALREADY DEAD (Book #5)
ALREADY TAKEN (Book #6)
ALREADY CHOSEN (Book #7)
ALREADY LOST (Book #8)
ALREADY HIS (Book #9)
ALREADY LURED (Book #10)
ALREADY COLD (Book #11)

EUROPEAN VOYAGE COZY MYSTERY SERIES

MURDER (AND BAKLAVA) (Book #1)
DEATH (AND APPLE STRUDEL) (Book #2)
CRIME (AND LAGER) (Book #3)
MISFORTUNE (AND GOUDA) (Book #4)
CALAMITY (AND A DANISH) (Book #5)
MAYHEM (AND HERRING) (Book #6)

ADELE SHARP MYSTERY SERIES

LEFT TO DIE (Book #1)
LEFT TO RUN (Book #2)
LEFT TO HIDE (Book #3)
LEFT TO KILL (Book #4)
LEFT TO MURDER (Book #5)
LEFT TO ENVY (Book #6)
LEFT TO LAPSE (Book #7)
LEFT TO VANISH (Book #8)
LEFT TO HUNT (Book #9)
LEFT TO FEAR (Book #10)
LEFT TO PREY (Book #11)
LEFT TO LURE (Book #12)
LEFT TO CRAVE (Book #13)
LEFT TO LOATHE (Book #14)
LEFT TO HARM (Book #15)
LEFT TO RUIN (Book #16)

THE AU PAIR SERIES
ALMOST GONE (Book#1)
ALMOST LOST (Book #2)
ALMOST DEAD (Book #3)

ZOE PRIME MYSTERY SERIES
FACE OF DEATH (Book#1)
FACE OF MURDER (Book #2)
FACE OF FEAR (Book #3)
FACE OF MADNESS (Book #4)
FACE OF FURY (Book #5)
FACE OF DARKNESS (Book #6)

A JESSIE HUNT PSYCHOLOGICAL SUSPENSE SERIES
THE PERFECT WIFE (Book #1)
THE PERFECT BLOCK (Book #2)
THE PERFECT HOUSE (Book #3)
THE PERFECT SMILE (Book #4)
THE PERFECT LIE (Book #5)
THE PERFECT LOOK (Book #6)
THE PERFECT AFFAIR (Book #7)
THE PERFECT ALIBI (Book #8)
THE PERFECT NEIGHBOR (Book #9)
THE PERFECT DISGUISE (Book #10)
THE PERFECT SECRET (Book #11)
THE PERFECT FAÇADE (Book #12)
THE PERFECT IMPRESSION (Book #13)
THE PERFECT DECEIT (Book #14)
THE PERFECT MISTRESS (Book #15)
THE PERFECT IMAGE (Book #16)
THE PERFECT VEIL (Book #17)
THE PERFECT INDISCRETION (Book #18)
THE PERFECT RUMOR (Book #19)
THE PERFECT COUPLE (Book #20)
THE PERFECT MURDER (Book #21)
THE PERFECT HUSBAND (Book #22)
THE PERFECT SCANDAL (Book #23)
THE PERFECT MASK (Book #24)
THE PERFECT RUSE (Book #25)
THE PERFECT VENEER (Book #26)
THE PERFECT PEOPLE (Book #27)

THE PERFECT WITNESS (Book #28)

CHLOE FINE PSYCHOLOGICAL SUSPENSE SERIES

NEXT DOOR (Book #1)
A NEIGHBOR'S LIE (Book #2)
CUL DE SAC (Book #3)
SILENT NEIGHBOR (Book #4)
HOMECOMING (Book #5)
TINTED WINDOWS (Book #6)

KATE WISE MYSTERY SERIES

IF SHE KNEW (Book #1)
IF SHE SAW (Book #2)
IF SHE RAN (Book #3)
IF SHE HID (Book #4)
IF SHE FLED (Book #5)
IF SHE FEARED (Book #6)
IF SHE HEARD (Book #7)

THE MAKING OF RILEY PAIGE SERIES

WATCHING (Book #1)
WAITING (Book #2)
LURING (Book #3)
TAKING (Book #4)
STALKING (Book #5)
KILLING (Book #6)

RILEY PAIGE MYSTERY SERIES

ONCE GONE (Book #1)
ONCE TAKEN (Book #2)
ONCE CRAVED (Book #3)
ONCE LURED (Book #4)
ONCE HUNTED (Book #5)
ONCE PINED (Book #6)
ONCE FORSAKEN (Book #7)
ONCE COLD (Book #8)
ONCE STALKED (Book #9)
ONCE LOST (Book #10)
ONCE BURIED (Book #11)
ONCE BOUND (Book #12)
ONCE TRAPPED (Book #13)

ONCE DORMANT (Book #14)
ONCE SHUNNED (Book #15)
ONCE MISSED (Book #16)
ONCE CHOSEN (Book #17)

MACKENZIE WHITE MYSTERY SERIES

BEFORE HE KILLS (Book #1)
BEFORE HE SEES (Book #2)
BEFORE HE COVETS (Book #3)
BEFORE HE TAKES (Book #4)
BEFORE HE NEEDS (Book #5)
BEFORE HE FEELS (Book #6)
BEFORE HE SINS (Book #7)
BEFORE HE HUNTS (Book #8)
BEFORE HE PREYS (Book #9)
BEFORE HE LONGS (Book #10)
BEFORE HE LAPSES (Book #11)
BEFORE HE ENVIES (Book #12)
BEFORE HE STALKS (Book #13)
BEFORE HE HARMS (Book #14)

AVERY BLACK MYSTERY SERIES

CAUSE TO KILL (Book #1)
CAUSE TO RUN (Book #2)
CAUSE TO HIDE (Book #3)
CAUSE TO FEAR (Book #4)
CAUSE TO SAVE (Book #5)
CAUSE TO DREAD (Book #6)

KERI LOCKE MYSTERY SERIES

A TRACE OF DEATH (Book #1)
A TRACE OF MURDER (Book #2)
A TRACE OF VICE (Book #3)
A TRACE OF CRIME (Book #4)
A TRACE OF HOPE (Book #5)

Made in the USA
Middletown, DE
06 September 2023